Che Mon Amour

WERNER ORTMÜLLER

Che Mon Amour

a novel

Bibliographical information of the Deutsche Nationalbibliothek

[German National Library]

The Deutsche Nationalbibliothek [German National Library] has

registered this publication in the German National Bibliography;

detailed bibliographical data may be accessed online at

http://dnb.dnb.de.

© 2018 Werner Ortmüller

Typesetting, cover design, production and publishing:

BoD – Books on Demand

ISBN: 978-3-7460-5377-6

Prolog

Gently a hand
passed over
their backs,
a form
derived from
the music of the spheres,
bringing just the barest hint
of hope.

Chapter I

Traveling at adventurous speed, the jeep hurtled along the bumpy country road. We were well shaken up. I had the feeling that my stomach was protesting at every moment. The breakfast we had eaten at a four star hotel in the Bolivian capital, La Paz, threatened to be violently disgorged onto the jeep's dusty windshield.

We were a small group of European journalists. Straight after breakfast, an army helicopter had flown us to Quebrada del Yuro. Here a Bolivian army officer showed us the spot where a bitter battle had taken place. This was where the legendary Comandante Ernesto Rafael Guevara de la Serna, known as "Che Guevara", was thought to have taken nine bullets in his body on 8 October 1967. On the following day the Bolivian military conveyed the body to the Señor de Malta hospital in Vallegrande. The mortal remains of the revolutionary, having been washed and embalmed by nursing staff and two German nuns, were laid on a bier. This in turn rested on a cement trough.

My name is Monique Cottillard. I am a journalist, working for the French weekly Le Temps. I have been given the job of looking into the circumstances which led to Che's violent death.

The room was stiflingly hot. The air smelt of sweat and decomposition, an aura emanating from the body which had been only superficially embalmed. When I saw the cadaverous face of Che, framed with disheveled dark brown strands, and the bullet riddled body – one leg almost completely severed – I was gripped by a feverish cold chill. I felt I was about to fall into a faint, but my colleagues supported me firmly, preventing me from collapsing. My Italian colleague, Francesco Mororelli, asked me, "Mademoiselle, would you like us to take you outside?"

"No thank you, it was just a momentary thing – I'll be feeling better directly," I answered. It was as if the dead man wanted to speak to me – yes, he was actually smiling at me, while the cameras flashed and clicked.

"*Mi pequeño cordero* – my little lamb – you don't have to be sorry on my account, it's all turned out just the way I wanted: today a myth has been created, the myth of Che the god, whose spirit will accompany all future revolutionaries, whom legions of the poor of the whole world will venerate as a saint. Today it all comes true, as I always predicted to you that it would." So that was how this despicable megalomaniac talked to me! I had always hated it when he called me his "little lamb" – after all I am a working woman, I have always had to work to support myself, I've been independent ever since I was a little girl. Yes, I had known Comandante Ernesto Guevara de la Serna, aka Che, very well. I had hated him and I had loved him – loved him so much that I would have laid down my life for him. Che was married but he always had one or more girls on the side, being as he was a proper South American macho. He was so very macho, in a hurtful and arrogant way, that there were times when I really wanted to kill him. I often thought I didn't ever want to see him again. But whenever he sent me one of his brief encrypted messages, I would take the next plane to the place where he happened to be. Only on Cuba did I never visit him, as on that island the walls had ears.

It must have been in 1963 when our weekly sent me to Algiers on the first anniversary of Algerian independence, to report on the event. My uncle Albert, who was also the editor of the journal, thought that in Algiers a pretty French girl might meet with less reserve than a male colleague would. I left the official press room of the hotel where the Algerian prime minister Ben Bella had been telling journalists from all over the world about his political ideas for the coming years. Ben Bella had not only touched on the problems of his country, he had also spoken about the future of the non-aligned nations. But it wasn't the Prime Minister's divagations that made the greatest impression on the assembled journalists – it was the speech of the Cuban revolutionary Che Guevara, who delivered a blistering attack on the Soviet Union.

He accused the USSR of doing too little to help the undeveloped nations, and of being covertly in league with imperialism. His actual words were: "When we create this kind of relationship between the two groups of nations, we have to admit that the socialist countries are in a certain sense the lackeys of imperialist exploitation!"

No doubt about it, this was strong stuff.

Later at the press conference Che reiterated his complaints about the Soviet Union: "The socialist countries have the moral obligation to put an end to their tacit complicity with the exploitative western nations."

The press conference was over, and Che had spoken at length and in detail, accusing both global powers of neglecting the undeveloped countries. The People's Republic of China, on the other hand, was praised for its aid to Cuba. After this Che immediately made for the rest rooms and had an asthma attack. I entered them just a moment after he did.

I got myself out of the press room of the hotel and made my way to the wash basins of the ladies' toilets, resplendent with white marble. I heard a loud groaning and gasping coming from one of the cubicles, as if somebody were having a choking fit.

"*Avez-vous besoin d'aide?*" I called out in French – "Do you need help?" And then, "Shall I get a doctor?" No answer. I repeated the question in Spanish, but could make no sense of the response. So I decided to open the door, and finally managed to do so with some considerable effort. There was blood all over the floor and the toilet bowl. A man in an olive green uniform was rolling in it from side to side, while frantically gasping for breath.

He had striking masculine features, and in spite of all the blood I recognized who it was lying on the marble floor. It was the legendary Comandante Che Guevara, who gasped as he turned in my direction: "*No, no médico, yo tengo inhalar!*" – "No, no doctor, I need to inhale!"

He must be having an asthma attack. Che managed to explain that I should fetch his inhaler from his hotel room, he would be better in no time. He gave me his diplomat's pass and a silver colored metal tag, stamped with the Cuban flag and the image of the Cuban prime minister Fidel Castro. It had the Roman numeral III on the back. "Show these things to the soldiers on guard outside my suite and explain to them that you need to fetch the inhaler, as you're a good friend of mine. That and not a word more!" the Comandante insisted.

I took myself off to the fourth floor of the hotel and explained to the soldiers on guard what I needed to do. After a short wait I was given a small package, with which I returned as quickly as possible to the ladies' wash rooms.

Che was waiting impatiently for his inhaler. He put it to his mouth and sucked the soothing medicine deeply into his lungs. In just a few minutes he was feeling better, and with my help was able to stand up.

"Mademoiselle, please excuse my momentary condition. I am afraid I had an asthma attack which compelled me to visit the toilets. I got the rooms mixed up and so ended up in the Ladies. I owe you my profoundest thanks for rescuing me in this emergency." He introduced himself with his correct name, though without mentioning his title. I told him my name, telling him that I was a correspondent working for the French weekly Le Temps. He didn't seem too happy about this, immediately suspecting the threat of exposure by some organ of the press. I put his mind at rest, explaining to him that my journal didn't indulge in primitive sensationalism. Le Temps was a serious political weekly. Che promised me an interview, if I would only help him to get away from this inhospitable place and make him human again. We crept out together, taking a service elevator to reach my small suite, far removed from Che's accommodation in the same hotel. "My guys don't need to be told about my little mishap, as they do like to gossip. By the time the story reaches my friend Fidel Castro, the mouse will have turned into a monster."

On reaching my suite, Che first of all went to the bathroom to clean himself up. He asked me to get him a sheet, which he wrapped around himself. I tried meanwhile to get the bloodstains out of his uniform. Sitting in my club chair and draped in bedlinen, Che looked less like a legendary revolutionary than a Roman senator. Che asked if it was OK for him to get something from the minibar. I said Yes at once. I said he should make the same drink for me that he was fixing for himself, which he took the liberty of doing. Of course it was some kind of Caribbean concoction, involving white rum, Coke and a dash of lemon juice.

I wanted to toast Che with best wishes for his speedy recovery, but he forestalled me with the following words: "I raise my glass to a brave Frenchwoman who comes from the motherland of all revolutions. I drink to the enchanting Monique, to whom I owe my life." Surprised by the flamboyant compliment, I turned red like a teenager and drained my glass in one go. Che immediately refilled it, and lit up one of his Cuban cigars. He had previously asked politely if it was all right for him to smoke.

His entire behavior was notably cultivated – not raw or primitive, such as one is inclined to associate with revolutionaries. I recalled internal news reports which had documented Che's history. He came from a cultured Argentinian family, had completed medical studies but never practiced as a doctor, deciding to dedicate himself to politics.

He asked me to call his security boss for him, as the guy always wanted to be kept posted about the current location of his Minister of Industry. When the Cuban security services answered, I passed the receiver to Che. He told his people that he was in a suite of the hotel, and was just giving an interview to an important French paper. This was going to take place in a private setting. Then he gave utterance to words that took me slightly aback. I did after all speak sufficient Spanish to understand what he was saying.

"I am just gazing into a pair of beautiful green eyes, and would like to be better acquainted with the *señorita* they belong to." Che anticipated my protest with the following words: "Mademoiselle Monique, I would not want to be importunate, I am just trying to pacify my security officers, who otherwise might get the idea of searching the hotel for me. Since the big international crisis last year, my security officers have been acting like crazy sometimes – they are always worrying that a Cuban politician might be kidnapped to hold the country to ransom. I must once again ask you to forgive my inappropriate remark."

This made me see his words in a rather different light. Of course I was well aware of the waves the Cuban missile crisis had made all over the world. At the time it looked as if a serious confrontation between the two superpowers, the USA and the USSR, was going to take place.

The USSR had stationed long range rockets on Cuba, which could have been fitted with atomic warheads. This meant that America's major cities, including the capital, were directly threatened by Soviet missiles. The American President, John F. Kennedy, delivered an ultimatum, calling for the long range rockets to be removed. Moreover the Soviet freighters carrying the rocket components, which were sailing for Cuba, should turn back immediately, otherwise American military operations would be inevitable. The long range bombers stationed around the USSR were on the point of dropping their atom bombs on Soviet territory. The world teetered on the brink of conflict until the Soviet head of state, Nikita Khrushchev, backed down and withdrew the rockets.

So a global atomic catastrophe had been only a hair's breadth away. The USSR thought it was in the right, as it felt encircled by NATO, in view of the fact that the western powers had positioned rockets all around the Soviet Union. In October 1962 the Soviets thought the time had come to engage in countermeasures.

I asked Che if he would like to tell me a bit about this unfortunate missile project. Or should the chapter finally be considered closed? Che told me that he was aware today that this plan of stationing rockets on Cuba had not been a good idea. It had been a case of the Soviet Union wanting to make a show of military strength against the USA, and going just a step too far. The USSR had come to an accommodation with the USA, without having first consulted its ally Cuba. "I am still of the opinion that our struggle must start with the oppressed masses, it is the masses who will change the capitalist system through revolutionary movements," the Comandante observed. "But wouldn't you like me to tell you something about my life? Perhaps then you will have a better understanding of my motives." Of course his life history would be highly interesting, and perhaps I could include some elements of current politics in the interview, I thought.

"I was born on 14 June 1928, as the son of the plantation owner Ernesto Guevara Lynch and his wife Celia de la Serna, in Rosario – that's in Argentina. I had my first asthma attack when I was two. As my attacks become more frequent, my family moved to the Alta Gracia region, not far from Córdoba. To my parents' disappointment, my health did not improve. My mother Celia had an aristocratic background. She was a very educated woman, who taught me French and put me in touch with culture. I had an uncommonly close relationship with her. Celia explained the world to me. Our extensive library, which included the works Marx and Engels, was my favorite place to hang out from the age of ten. This was where I found the important political books that interested me. To strengthen my debilitated body I did a lot of sport. And I went on lots of cycling and hiking trips with my younger brother Roberto. Later on I became a passionate rugby player. But because of the handicap of my illness, I didn't make it into the first team of the first division of the Atletico Atalaya sports club. A top class athlete can't keep taking time out to rush to the changing room where he's left his inhaler.

"In the year 1945 I met my first love. She was a girl who came from one of the richest families in Córdoba. She was called María del Carmen Ferreyra; her friends called her Chichina. She was exceptionally beautiful and aristocratic. Her family were absolutely incapable of understanding what their cultivated highborn daughter saw in me. I came from a destitute family, dressed shabbily or casually, I just was not on the same level as these rich elitists. When I was invited to visit them and saw these bored dandies in their expensive outfits, I was constantly provoked to contradict them. Only Chichina stuck by me when her numerous admirers spoke of me disparagingly. I wrote her love poems, which always gave her a lot of pleasure. She kept the poems in a locked casket.

"There came a time when Chichina wanted to teach me how to dance. As you are perhaps aware, the tango is something very special in Argentina. When a couple gracefully moves to these romantic rhythms, it's often the vertical prelude to a later physical conjunction.

"Unfortunately I am a completely unmusical person, I have no sense of timing, and so Chichina's well meant dancing instruction was wasted on me. We loved one another for almost a decade. But we had to separate in the end, because the class difference between us was too extreme."

"Can you still not dance the tango?" I heard myself ask the Comandante.

"That's right, my dancing ineptitude has remained incurable right up to the present day."

"Shan't we just give it a try?" I asked my visitor, not thinking the question to be in any way flirtatious or a come-on.

The Comandante stood up and made a little bow, like a beginner in dancing class, and then trod the boards around the room in a stumbling demonstration. I hummed a tune which I hoped sounded like a tango rhythm, until we suddenly landed on the hotel bed. Che's bedlinen toga had shown it had a mind of its own, he was lying naked alongside me, and we both laughed at his plight.

When he started to stroke me tenderly, almost shyly, I shrank back in the first instant but then let it happen. No doubt the cocktails had taken effect, as I can't say that I put up very much resistance.

I whispered to Che something that sounded like "But Comandante, you are still unwell." The legendary South American only laughed: "Mademoiselle, I have never felt better than I do at this moment, when I can be so close to you."

As a lover, Che was anything but a beginner. He took his time, with repeated stroking and tender lip contact, carrying me away onto a cloud of bliss. His heart and mine beat in excited harmony, our breath became ever more vehement, until a mighty flood of light terminated this heartfelt fusion of two souls.

Later, still heated, we were lying alongside each other. Che told me that he had actually chosen to study medicine in order to help people. Another reason was his asthmatic condition – he had hoped to develop a serum of his own that would be a cure. "As you had the opportunity of observing, success has been denied me," he said with an air of resignation. "At the moment you don't seem to have any kind of health problem," I said sleepily. I must have dropped off at the same moment.

When I woke up, it was already broad daylight. I opened the window and heard the noisy bustle of the oriental market, which was held close to the hotel.

Gradually the embraces and tender encounters of the previous night came back to me, and a pleasant shudder ran down my back.

It wasn't generally my kind of thing, this, to sleep with just any man who crossed my path in a hotel. But what happened last night had been somehow special.

At the Sorbonne, as a young student, I had even been thought unapproachable – people said I would end up as an old maid. Later I went out with a few men, but the relationships did not last long. Until, that is I had met Gérard two years before, with whom I started a quite loose relationship. We lived in separate apartments and met up two or three times a week to do something together. Gérard had not given any indication so far that our relationship might develop into something more permanent. There was no doubt that apart from me he had intimate encounters with other women, and he didn't want to give them up.

A room service waiter knocked on the door and asked for permission to enter. I rapidly pulled on my dressing gown, as I had answered his question by saying "*Entrez*". The hotel employee wheeled in a two level serving trolley, on which an opulent breakfast was laid out. "An anonymous guest has ordered this for you, Mademoiselle, and wishes you *bon appétit*." I was bowled over by this generous breakfast. Of course it was not hard to think who this anonymous guest might be. A slim vase holding a dark red rose stood in the middle of the serving trolley, surrounded by every culinary delicacy imaginable. I gave the waiter a tip, and opened the accompanying note. Che thanked me again for my readiness to help and apologized for his absence, as he had had to get to the airport very early to return home to Cuba with the rest of his delegation. "I regret that the interview could not be completed. By way of an apology, there will be a surprise waiting for you when you get back to your publishers in Paris. Warmest wishes, from your Che."

After having enjoyed an ample breakfast, I packed quickly, still in a good mood, so that I would be in time for the plane to Paris. Before I left the hotel room, I looked around one last time to see if I had forgotten anything, and discovered the ashtray with Che's stubbed out cigar ends. I put them all in an empty pill box, not wanting to lose them for the world. Something of the strong aroma that Che's Havana cigars had left behind them still hung in the air of the room.

Privately, I told myself I was a complete idiot. How could a woman raised to be independent get such romantic notions into her head?

Years after Che's death, when I had suffered a disappointment or when something particularly nice had happened, I would take the pill box out of my desk, hold the cigar ends in my hand and smell the small, still fragrant, almost black stumps which reminded me of my time with the legendary revolutionary.

Chapter II

When on the following morning I entered the building of our Paris publishing house, our concierge Reymon, whose hair had turned gray over many years of service, greeted me with the words, "Have you had a pleasant trip, Mademoiselle?" Without waiting for an answer from me, he went on, "Your uncle is attending a reception at the American embassy. When he gets back, he'll be giving you a call."

In the anteroom of my office my secretary told me all that had been going on at the company in my absence. Dear Lyselle was completely over the moon about the letter that had come for me from Algiers. "It's from the Cuban Minister of Industry, the legendary Che Guevara," she called after me, her voice quivering with something that sounded like admiration.

I sat down at my desk and opened the envelope, in which was a typewritten article for the press. The article gave an overview of the current world political situation, along with visions of a future of social justice, which would not be attainable without revolutionary struggle; then there were some details of Guevara's earlier life. All this had been sent to me by Che.

The entire article was written in excellent French, and was practically ready for printing. I only needed to adapt the format for our newspaper, add a suitable photo of the revolutionary – and there was a press article that looked entirely respectable.

Uncle Albert – still in the tails he had worn at the reception – came into my office to say hello. "Monique, it's good to see you back! How was your flight? Did you manage to see the Cuban minister?"

I answered all his questions in the order in which they had been asked, and then showed him Che's article and the notes I had made at the hotel.

My uncle was delighted with the material I had given him. "I say, Monique, we'll turn it into a whole series of articles. You must have made a tremendous impression on the minister, to be given this preferential treatment. You stick with him at all times, and give us up close and personal reports. The man is a living legend!"

The old man was jubilant. But if my dear uncle had only known, how up close and personal I had been with Che in the hotel... He would never have credited it.

No doubt Uncle Albert had been a chivalrous gallant in his day, but since Aunt Claudine died he had been living alone, apart from a housekeeper and his driver and aged factotum Emile, at his house outside Paris. Every morning he had Emile drive him to the publishing house, returning in the evening in the same manner to Fontainebleau.

I couldn't help thinking of Che. What might he be doing at this very moment? Well, he must have returned to Havana by this time. No doubt to his wife and family. Family meant a lot to these South Americans, of course. As for me, my parents and my older brother François had died prematurely, so I had never known what real family life was like.

It would be very unfair to my aunt and uncle to say

that they had not raised me like their own daughter. They had done everything imaginable to replace my mother and father. But it just wasn't quite the same as having parents.

How did Ernesto Guevara de la Serna, born in Argentina, achieve fame as a legendary revolutionary?

I gave our archivist a call, and asked to be sent all the documents we had relating to Che Guevara.

In January 1953 Ernesto Guevara and the love of his life had split up. The lifestyles of the two young people were just too different. Chichina expected, while being with Ernesto, that she would be able to carry on the same luxurious life that she had enjoyed in the bosom of her parents on their big hacienda. Ernesto was a medical student, and on qualifying wanted to help the most shunned and unfortunate people in this world – lepers. On his trip round South America, the idealistic Che had met these unhappy creatures.

As a doctor working at a leper colony, he would hardly have been able to offer his future life partner any kind of elevated lifestyle. Before the end of the year 1953 he qualified as a physician specialized in dermatology, entitling him to practice as a doctor and surgeon.

With a view to getting over the pain of parting from Chichina, Ernesto went on another road trip through South America. At the time he vowed that he would never return to Argentina until the whole world was talking about him.

Just at this time a hitherto unknown Cuban student by the name of Fidel Castro tried to storm one of the barracks of the dictator Batista. The attack was a total failure. Castro's desperate followers, a small bunch of undaunted fighters, were mown down by Batista's soldiers like standing corn.

Fulgencio Batista was a total dictator, of a degree of awfulness rarely seen in South America. Relying on every method of repression, including torture, he kept his political opponents firmly under his thumb.

This grim dictator could safely count on American support, seeing that the Cuban capital, Havana, was practically a flophouse for well heeled Americans. In Cuba you could get anything for dollars – drugs, casino games, prostitutes and sexual perversities of all kinds.

At that time Ernesto Guevara and his two traveling companions, Ricardo Rojo and Carlos Ferrer, were on the shores of Lake Titicaca – a vast body of water, situated in the Andes at an altitude of almost four thousand meters. Ernesto's passion for archeology blazed up in him again, as he took pictures of the columns and walls which the Inca stone masons had built without mortar centuries ago.

It was Rojo who set out to open his idealistic friend Ernesto's eyes to the realities of South American politics.

In Ecuador's biggest port, Guayaquil, they met three more Argentinians, students who like them were on an adventure trip. A civil war was raging in Colombia. Consequently the Colombian consul refused to recognize the visa which would have entitled them to travel through the country.

But Rojo had a better idea. A letter from the Chilean

socialist Salvador Allende opened doors for the young men, enabling them to continue their journey by ship. Rojo persuaded Ernesto Guevara to visit Guatemala. There was a serious revolution happening there, he said, which Che wouldn't want to miss on any account.

While they were traveling Ernesto found time to write a few articles about the Inca sites, seen from a romantic/idealistic standpoint. But the important thing was that he earned a bit of money from a Panama journal, so helping to finance his further travels. In Panama City Ernesto met the leaders of the "Caribbean Legion". These revolutionary politicians of the left wanted to fight the many dictatorships that existed in the Caribbean region, and transform them into socialist or communist regimes.

The young medic was fascinated by Juan Bosch, who came from the Dominican Republic. Bosch had been known in South America in the past more as a literary figure, so he and the young Argentinian had a lot to talk about.

In San José, the capital of Costa Rica, Ernesto Guevara heard the name of Fidel Castro for the first time. Survivors of Castro's band reported the torture and shooting of innocent people by the frightful Cuban dictator Batista. More and more young people, they said, were determined to topple this savage regime. Batista's terror had the total support of the USA, the Cubans told him. As an idealist Ernesto had always felt resentful toward the USA, and his resentment progressively grew beyond all bounds. Ernesto's friend Alberto Granado had traveled on to Venezuela, but he himself wanted to stay in Guatemala and join the socialist groups supporting the democratically elected President Jacobo Árbenz Guzmán. This freely elected president had had the audacity to push through a land reform whereby plots left uncultivated would be repossessed, indemnification being paid to the owners. This had particular implications for the American United Fruit Company, which owned large tracts of land in Central America. Of course the USA was not going to stand by and let this happen. At the end of 1953 the CIA was on the brink of launching an attempted putsch.

Ernesto had not been long in Guatemala, when another woman entered his life. This was the Peruvian socialist Hilda Gadea, who became his lover as well as a kind of mother figure. In quite a touching way, she looked after the young Argentinian and helped him find work.

When Colonel Castillo Armas, with financial backup from the CIA, invaded Guatemala from Honduras, Ernesto volunteered to join the "Young Brigades" supporting Árbenz, the president in office. He was in the capital of Guatemala when it was bombarded. As a target for enemy bombs, he experienced for the first time the sense of his own invulnerability. It must have been a kind of rush of euphoria which came over him, and would do so repeatedly in later life. We could almost say that Ernesto Guevara was always running after this deceptive sense of elation.

Under pressure from his own military, President Árbenz was forced to resign. At the same time some friends of Ernesto's were arrested. These included his partner Hilda Gadea.

After a wait of two months, Ernesto obtained a visa for Mexico. He wanted above all to meet the leader of the Cuban revolutionaries, Fidel Castro.

Now released from jail, his partner followed him, and the couple got married in August 1955 close to Mexico City. In February 1956 Hilda Gadea gave birth to a girl, whom they called Hilda Beatriz.

Guevara met Fidel Castro in September 1955. Night after night they sat up discussing the political situation in Cuba and in the whole of South America. After this it was clear to Ernesto Guevara that he should join the Cuban guerilla fighters.

On a farm close to Mexico City the revolutionaries were trained in close combat skills by Colonel Alberto Chalco, a veteran of the Spanish Civil War. The training was anything but a bed of roses. They practiced shooting, carried out forced marches and learned how to defend themselves at close quarters.

In spite of his asthma, Guevara was one of the best solo fighters. On the mountain slopes exceptional efforts were called for from all the guerillas. Ernesto Guevara did more than was asked of him, and helped his comrades wherever he could.

His fellow fighters soon gave him the nickname of "Che", meaning something like "buddy" or "pal". Guevara was pleased with the soubriquet, seeing it as a badge of honor. It was clear to him that he would bear this name till the end of his life. Soon the authorities found out about the training camp, and Castro's partisans were arrested and jailed. After two weeks all of them were released again except for Guevara and Calixto García, who remained in prison. But Castro did not leave his supporters in the lurch, procuring their liberty with some judicious payments in the right quarters.

Castro waited for them near Tuxpan, on the Gulf of Mexico. He had acquired an aged motorized yacht and got hold of weapons.

With eighty-two men on board, the motorized yacht "Granma", under Fidel Castro's command, put out to sea from the Mexican port on 25 November 1956.

Heavily overloaded, the ship ran aground two kilometers off the coast in Cuba's eastern province, Oriente, not far from the Sierra Maestra. They were spotted by aircraft of the Cuban airforce, and immediately came under fire. Cuban ground troops loyal to the government had also noticed the guerilla band. A battle took place in the neighborhood of Alegría de Pío, and most of the rebels were killed, wounded or captured.

Guevara too was grazed in the neck by a bullet, and was so seriously hurt that he thought his last hour had come.

The fifteen rebels remaining tried to stay alive in the Sierra Maestra, a heavily forested mountainous region.

Castro assessed the state of their weaponry and provisions. The situation was devastating. All the same he announced optimistically, "Seven guns. Now we are bound to win the war!"

Guevara's health was very poor. He had to struggle with repeated asthma attacks. As a result he was once separated from his group. He had already had to hand over his gun to another comrade. Later he noted in his diary, "These days were some of the bitterest I ever experienced in the mountains."

Fidel Castro succeeded in making contact with the resistance organization led by Frank País, the "26 July Movement". They sent him fighters to swell his ranks and replenished his supply of weapons.

Castro ordered his guerillas to look after wounded enemy soldiers, and let them go free. This was part of his psychology of war. He hoped the rebels would win the sympathy of the population and undermine the fighting strength of their opponents.

Guevara too gave medical treatment to enemy combatants, to the best of his ability. He also treated the local peasant population.

He showed himself so fearless in combat that his comrades urged him not to throw his life away.

Castro raised him to the rank of Comandante. He was given a small red star, which in later years he always wore on his beret. He was made responsible for leading a column of his own. This appointment, of which he was very proud, made Guevara the number two in the rebel army after Castro.

After a number of skirmishes, the rebel army had made themselves masters of the entire Sierra Maestra. They needed to set up an effective supply and information network. The most important elements were a hospital, a poultry farm and clothing supply stations. A small bakery was another essential. Likewise the rebels tried to manufacture their own munitions. The key man on whom it all turned was always Ernesto Guevara.

He discussed land reform with the local peasantry. He also taught them reading and writing, along with his fellow guerillas. He founded his own radio broadcasting station, "Radio Rebelde", and issued a newspaper under the title "El Cubano Libre" – the Free Cuban.

People's admiration for the Comandante grew and grew. Guevara did not try to give the impression of omniscience and omnipotence. He treated those under him, who were simple peasants, as human beings with equal rights.

Gradually the "Che myth", which would accompany him all his life, was created. He himself believed so firmly in his own transfiguration that he later thought himself to be invulnerable and invincible. This sojourn in the Sierra Maestra must always have been a positive memory for Che. For a short while, rebels and peasants were living together in this forested landscape in what was practically a commune. This was how Che imagined a later communist society would be.

In April 1958, the Cuban dictator Batista got ready for a new offensive. It was destined to be his last. Some ten thousand soldiers were ordered to surround the Sierra Maestra. They reconquered a large part of the territory held by the guerillas, without deriving any decisive benefit from it.

Meanwhile the guerillas, with their three hundred armed fighters, inflicted serious defeats on Batista's army from time to time, so that the soldiers retreated from the mountains weary of fighting and with their tail between their legs.

Castro now had the upper hand, he sensed. He planned to complete his conquest of the island by fielding three columns – under his brother Raúl, Guevara and Camilo Cienfuegos. Che's column was a hundred and forty men strong. Many of them were young lads who would have followed their Comandante through the fire. They marched to the point of exhaustion, overcame hunger and thirst, were strafed by enemy aircraft and then found themselves at the gates of the biggest city in central Cuba, the provincial capital of Santa Clara with 150,000 inhabitants.

Four thousand soldiers loyal to Batista and splendidly equipped, faced four hundred guerilla fighters.

At the end of December Che gave the signal for the attack. Within three days his fighters had occupied one district after another. It was one of the bloodiest episodes of the entire battle.

Even when the enemy was reinforced by an armored train which came to their assistance, the guerilleros were unstoppable.

Guevara had made the crucial contribution to this victory. He drove his men tirelessly, but was always himself in the forefront. He he was here and there and everywhere – mostly in the thick of the combat.

He had become the legendary "Comandante Che".

But at the same time the revolutionary hero had developed a massive tendency to overestimate himself. Victories, he was convinced, could only be achieved through strength of will, morality and discipline.

He underestimated the political and organizational support which had lent wings to the resistance in the Cuban cities, thinking it an insignificant factor. This fatal misjudgment would later lead, in the Congo and in Bolivia, to the defeat and final downfall of Comandante Che.

On New Year's Eve, 1959, the dictator Batista left Cuba for the Dominica Republic. And on 2 January 1959 Castro and his guerilleros entered Havana. He and his "barbudos" or bearded warriors were jubilantly welcomed by the local population. Che waited in the La Cabaña fortress, till he received an order from Castro to occupy the military headquarters. As a foreigner, Che was not allowed to be the first to penetrate the center of power – that was an honor reserved to the Cuban born Fidel Castro. But in a very short time Che was declared by law a Cuban citizen. On Castro's orders, he was made responsible for all judgments of the summary court. This court met between eight and nine in the morning, heard witnesses for the prosecution and the defense and then handed down the verdict. Most commonly it was a sentence of death, which would be carried out that same night. In the two months following Castro's seizure of power, several hundred people are thought to have been executed. The Cuban population held these measures to be largely justified, as something like twenty thousand people had been put to death under the brutal Batista regime.

Chapter III

Uncle Albert came to see me in my office, looking as if he had just had a personal visit from Santa Claus. After he had asked how my current projects were progressing, he casually asked, "Monique, how would you feel about a trip to the People's Republic of China?" It was like being struck by lightning – in those days, for western journalists, a visa to China was practically an impossibility. "Of course I'll go with you, Uncle Albert," I answered. "*Mais non*, Monique, you're going to Beijing on your own. Only one French journalist is allowed to accompany the Cuban delegation on their visit. My excellent contacts with the various embassies were enough to ensure that you, Monique, are the lucky winner. In Beijing the revolutionary Che Guevara will be meeting the leader of the most heavily populated country of the world. It's said that Che is very much impressed by Mao Tse-tung. He would like to forge closer links between Cuba and China, and you, my dear Monique, will be there to represent the entire French press. This means that your journal will be reporting exclusively on the progress of talks. Naturally, the other organs of the press will be briefed by you likewise. Now don't look so appalled, you should be pleased that you have been chosen to represent France," my uncle concluded with a laugh.

Of course I was delighted with the honor. But it was also a big responsibility to represent the entire French press abroad. At the same time, this totally unexpected opportunity of seeing Che again was very tempting.

How long was it since we had seen each other last? I counted the days. It must have been a good six months since our encounter in Algiers.

As soon as we arrived at the Beijing airport, our small group of international journalists was welcomed by an important representative of the Chinese government. A lady interpreter explained to us that each reporter would have two government officials assigned to him or her, in order to ensure our safety. My Italian colleague Roberto Bocci, who represented the La Stampa daily, whispered in my ear, "Welcome to the free People's Democracy of China – as of now, every step we make will be under surveillance."

A bus took us to our hotel – a splendid Victorian building which must have gone back to the colonial era. In the reception area we were again welcomed by the hotel manager. Two escorts were assigned to each of us, and they stuck with us like limpets whenever we indicated any intention of leaving the hotel.

I was surprised by the quantities of staff who were there to serve us, bowing constantly. Already on the trip to the hotel I had been struck by the numerous portraits of Mao Tse-tung. There was a Mao on every street corner, banners quoting his Thoughts were everywhere, and even at the hotel, in every room, there were several pictures of the Great Chairman.

My own "room", which was actually more like a suite, consisted of separate living and sleeping areas, along with a small kitchen niche.

I had hardly unpacked my suitcase and traveling bag when I heard a knock on the door. A hotel employee gave me to understand, bowing a lot in the process, that a certain Monsieur Cottillard was waiting for me.

Well now! Has my Uncle Albert come along after all? – that was my first reaction.

The bellhop accompanied me to the entrance to the bar, then disappeared again, still bowing repeatedly. He refused the tip I offered him, saying that the receipt of tips was absolutely forbidden to the staff. As I entered the bar, a figure in an olive green uniform was already approaching me rapidly.

"Hola, my French lass! I'm so pleased to see you again!" It was Ernesto Che Guevara.

I resisted the Cuban's hug half-heartedly. Actually I was quite taken aback to run into the revolutionary so soon. "Look, Monique, we're actually in the same hotel. Our delegation has got accommodation just a few floors up on the other side of this old pile." Before I could get my breath, he turned me on my own axis in front of the bar, so that I felt a little bit dizzy. "What can I get you? How about a Cuba Libre? Or would you prefer a glass of champagne? It's all compliments of the house, you know, as the members of our delegation are personal guests of Chairman Mao. You know what, Monique, tomorrow we are invited to the Beijing Opera, our delegation will be sitting in a box with Mao. I've been given a spare ticket. I was able to reserve a seat for you in a box to the side." At last I managed to get a word in edgeways: "I'm very happy to have the opportunity of experiencing the famous Beijing Opera at first hand."

The following evening, I was sitting by myself in the

big side box, and watched the gigantic theater gradually filling up.

The prevailing dress color was a uniform blue, worn by men as well as women. Not wanting to stand out, this evening I too was wearing a simple navy blue pant suit. The same color was predominant on the streets of Beijing. If I wore a brightly colored dress or pant suit, I would be instantly surrounded by a crowd of Chinese women wanting to feel the fabric of the "long-nose". "Long-nose" was what they called us Europeans. It's the same sort of thing as when we call Asiatics "slit-eyes". But our Chinese minders immediately intervened to prevent any contact between us and the Chinese population.

When Mao Tse-tung and a number of important functionaries entered the gigantic middle box, all the spectators rose to their feet and clapped. Che was sitting next to Mao in the box; behind them were several Cubans, along with other Chinese dignitaries.

After a second the high pitched sing-song and metallic chink of musical instruments were already getting on my nerves. What was worse, the stage was enveloped from time to time in clouds of some kind of incense, which irritated my throat to such a degree that I had to cough from time to time.

The dance numbers of the actors were outstanding. They delivered a truly artistic and masterly performance.

The plot of the opera, which of course took place in China's revolutionary era, can be quickly told. The young farmer's son Ling-San joins the revolutionary forces of Mao Tse-tung. Ling-San looks after the village's granaries. He loves the young peasant girl Lu-Ling, on whom the former landowner Lang-Lung has already cast a lustful eye. Clandestinely, the latter goes over to the Nationalist Chiang Kai-shek, and betrays the location of the granaries. The Nationalists take the young farmer's son Ling-San prisoner, burn down the granaries, and the wicked landowner kidnaps the peasant girl Lu-Ling. But the revolutionary supporters of Mao Tse-tung are already hard on the heels of the villainous landowner. The young farmer's son is released and can hold his beloved in his arms again, while the rentier will have to face the extreme penalty. The Nationalists flee in panic before the revolutionary peasant army of Mao Tse-tung. Every quarter of an hour, the entire theater ensemble lined up in front of a more than life-sized flower-garlanded image of the Great Chairman and applauded. The spectators applauded likewise, and the beneficently smiling Mao applauded back. After something like three hours, the curtain finally descended. But none of the spectators left the theater. After the artistes had been applauded at length, it was another half an hour or so before the Great Chairman left the premises. The whole audience remained respectfully standing, until Mao and all his guests had left their lavish box.

In the hotel bar, later on, Che asked me what impression I had formed of our Chinese hosts.

"To be perfectly honest, this big fuss they make over Mao seems a bit bizarre to me. Are the Chinese afraid of him, or do they really find him so fabulous that they have to keep groveling at his heels?"

"In China, Mao is a great popular hero and a wise party leader. His peasant army fought for decades, with its rudimentary equipment of hoes, shovels and clubs, against the superbly weaponed Nationalists under Chiang Kai-shek – whose army had been supplied by the Americans with everything they needed to win the war: guns, hand grenades, trucks and food supplies. They were supposed to be firming up the rotten system of the landed gentry. But the superhuman will of Mao drove the peasant army to ultimate victory. They captured weapons and munitions of all kinds. Their steadfastness and inflexibility demoralized the Nationalists. Chiang Kai-shek fled to the island of Formosa. Mao achieved a magnificent victory, which actually nobody had expected," said Che, putting me in the picture.

"He was not just the practitioner and organizer of the revolution," Che continued – "he was also the theoretician who defined the foundations, even while the civil war was still raging, for the establishment of a new Communist society. What was accomplished in Cuba in miniature has happened here, in this country with its ancient culture, on a massive scale. That is why we get on so well – the wise old revolutionary Mao, and the very young revolutionary Che Guevara. I would like to see closer cooperation between Cuba and the People's Republic of China, but Castro is completely counting on the Soviet Union. Mao wants to take the revolution to Central Africa, so as to educate the Africans to be proud and independent people, just like what he has achieved with the Chinese," he finished enthusiastically.

"Che, the Chinese are wonderfully friendly guys, but something here seems very strange to me. I wish I could read people's thoughts, when they can only exchange a few words with us. But any contact is prevented by our minders. Haven't you noticed how covetously the Chinese women look at my colorful pant suit or simple summer dress? These dear people could surely do with a bit more color in their clothes. And then, this whole cult of the person, of Mao, strikes me as a bit anachronistic. It reminds me of the old reports in the weeklies that showcased Hitler, Stalin or Mussolini. The Chinese move like puppets on strings. These blue ants aren't really free, and they are no way able to determine their own lives. There's always a functionary telling them what they can and can't do," I replied. As an ardent admirer of Mao Tse-tung, Che cannot have approved of my remarks – but he told me that tomorrow we were invited to the Forbidden City for a ceremonial banquet in honor of Chairman Mao Tsetung. The whole Cuban delegation and all the foreign journalists were invited.

"Come on, Monique! Look here, we don't want to be arguing all the time. We're only going to be together for three days and then it's the parting of the ways. Is your minibar still supplied? If not, I'll get them to bring a bottle of champagne to the room."

This South American certainly knew how to deal with women. His embraces, his tender whispers as he nibbled at my ear, instantly made me forget all the Maos and dictators of this world.

All the time he was in China, Che didn't have a single asthma attack. This was in part down to the peaceful and relaxed atmosphere of our Chinese hotel. The staff could tell what we wanted just by looking at us. For the time being I was together with the man I loved, who as he had done in Algiers carried me away into a transfigured world where wars and revolutions no longer existed. No man had ever taken me to such heights before, to this state of boundless happiness.

The following evening the Cuban delegation, along with all the accompanying journalists, were invited by the Great Chairman Mao Tse-tung to a ceremonial banquet. We were able to joint the select minority authorized to enter the Forbidden City. The name went back to the time of the Chinese imperial dynasties, when the general population had been forbidden, on pain of death, to set foot in this special quarter of Beijing. The ban had been strictly maintained under Mao's rule.

This evening, however, the former imperial palace and all the adjoining buildings were shining with the bright light cast by colored lanterns. Thousands of these luminaries had transformed the buildings, statues and paths into an unimaginable fairytale, an ocean of light.

Little barques rocked on the artificial ponds and canals, decked out with colored chains of light.

My Italian colleague and I were sitting at a table that was decorated with lots of brightly colored flowers.

Even the armrests of the chairs had been beautified with floral garlands.

Every table was waited on by two Chinese, who were there to take their orders. The courses were served by young Chinese girls who served the guests with great efficiency and some grace.

When Mao appeared on the terrace, all those present stood up and clapped. The Great Chairman clapped in response, and sat down at the head of the long table reserved for the Cuban delegation. Immediately two Chinese women were ready and waiting at the Mao's left hand, and two more to the right, to comply with his requests.

Che had already warned me to expect an impossible quantity of Chinese dishes. If I didn't think something was edible, I should just taste a forkful – the staff would remove the rest without batting an eyelid. The tables had been laid with chopsticks, as well as knives, forks and spoons.

The waiting staff kept filling our glasses with a lukewarm rice wine, which gradually rose to my head.

After courses of exotic food that seemed endless and some glasses of the rice wine, the guests were starting to let their hair down. A Chinese attendant rang a small bell for attention, and announced that the Great Chairman Mao Tse-tung would now deliver a short address.

Mao lavished praises on revolutionary Cuba and expressed the hope that a close partnership between Cuba and China would come to pass. Mao urged the western journalists to report objectively about the Middle Kingdom, as this people was currently engaged in a phase of renewal with the aim of making the Great Leap Forward.

The next item on the agenda was for all those present to migrate with their glasses from table to table, to toast each and every one of the guests, wish them all the best and then return to their seats. This, we were told, was an ancient Chinese custom.

So after we had all paraded round the banqueting hall in clockwise direction, and each of those present had toasted everyone else present, the Chinese who functioned as the bell ringer announced that now was the time when we would be permitted to tread the dance floor.

Che hurried over from the long table to claim a dance from me. The small orchestra struck up a melody that might just have been meant to resemble a tango. No doubt this was a gesture of politeness to the Cuban visitors. But at times I thought I recognized the transmogrified strains of the Beijing Opera. Che and I got through the dance as best we could.

A little while later, one of Mao's confidants approached our table and told me that the Great Chairman would like to dance with a representative of the western press. His choice had fallen on me – on this "charming flower from the motherland of the revolution".

Two waiters accompanied me to the place where Mao was sitting. He at once got up, and led me to the dance floor. All the other couples formed a circle around us, while Mao and I remained in the center of the circle. An indefinable melody began to play. Mao, who by Chinese standards was uncommonly tall, took me in his arms. We slithered over the parquet.

When the music came to a stop, there was a storm of applause. Presumably this was how his paladins tried to keep the boss in a good mood. Mao accompanied me back to my table. While one waiter bowed to me, the other waiter adjusted my seat.

Afterwards Che said to me, "You must have made a big impression on the great revolutionary leader, seeing that he personally escorted you back to your seat."

I riposted, "Mao has bad teeth, his breath is no better and he dances like Yogi Bear."

Later on I was visiting the toilets of the palace. Someone suddenly called my name: "Mademoiselle Cottillard, Mademoiselle Cottillard! I'm over here, behind the statue of the Warrior. Please stop just for a moment. Here's a press report for your newspaper. Mao is currently engaged in killing lots of his political opponents, or making them disappear for years into labor camps. What they call the 'Cultural Revolution' in this country is really nothing but the murder of hundreds of thousands of Chinese – teachers, authors, artists and party functionaries, even the state president, they have all been marked for execution. But the worst perpetrator is Mao's wife Jiang Qing. She is even more ruthless and power obsessed than her husband. Mao's abortive reform means that he has failed. Just look at this idiotic blast furnace campaign. They wanted to have a mini blast furnace in every back yard, to boost steel production. The steel produced was sub-standard, the whole thing was a disaster. Mao's agricultural reforms were even worse. Rice production has fallen year by year. Massive famines have been the result, with disastrous consequences for the population. To avoid being brought to book for this, Mao dreamed up the Cultural Revolution. School children and students, the 'Red Guard', so called, abduct innocent people from their homes and put them into massive concentration camps. If you so much as have a book about Confucius, Lao-Tse or Zhuangzi in your house, that's all they need to throw people in jail. If you have a pearl necklace or other article of jewelry in your possession, which may be a family heirloom, that could well be fatal. The military and the police watch all this murderous frenzy and do nothing about it. Many art treasures dating from the time of the imperial dynasties have been destroyed. Mademoiselle, please report about the terrible things going on our country! Now you must go please," instructed the voice, which was the voice of a woman and had been speaking excellent French.

Later on, in my hotel suite – Che had accompanied me as always – he asked me why I was so thoughtful. I said to him, "There are frightful things going on in this country, while we enjoy the fine life."

"It's just a revolutionary process in the Middle Kingdom which has to go on. Mao in his wisdom will know when the country can be restored to normality. He will lead it to shining shores. But let's not talk about politics now," Che went on. "Look, we've just got two days before we go back, each of us, to the everyday routine. My little lamb, shouldn't we raise a glass together and drink to improved Franco-Cuban relations?" He nodded in the direction of the king size hotel bed my suite had to offer.

"Mao is ruining this country, the Cultural Revolution does not exist, innocent people are being arrested and killed, your Great Chairman is a mass murderer," I hurled at him.

"But Monique, who has been telling you this nonsense? Of course a figure like Mao is going to have enemies, who would like to crush him if they could. You must have been talking to an American journalist, who still can't get over the defeat of Chiang Kai-shek."

"No, my informant was Chinese, and I intend to report in full to the French public about this unacceptable state of things."

"Don't do that, it may be just unchecked material serving the purposes of pure propaganda," said Che, trying to talk me around. "With an act of revolution, existing systems must give way – only so can the new and the lofty grow and develop. Only in this way can our lives, our culture and our history move in the right direction. All great personalities started by sweeping away the old corrupt system, and then later set up their free society on the basis of popular support. Lenin, Stalin, Hitler, Mao and Castro first of all excised the malignant carcinoma on the body of the people, in order to get the process of healing going. And that is exactly what is going on in the People's Republic of China. My little lamb, let's not always be talking about politics. I'll just take a look in your minibar to see if we could fix a drink. We only have two more days in this glorious country. Two days just for us," Che said insistently.

"I am *not* your little lamb, I am a professional woman, and right now I have no desire to go to bed with you. What outrages did you actually commit in the La Cabaña fortress?" I challenged him.

"It was Cuba, there was a revolution going on! You of all people should be familiar with this kind of thing, *Mademoiselle La Revolution*. What do you think it was like back then, with your bunch in France?"

"I thought that as a doctor you would have a humanist conscience. But what do you do? You condemn something like fifteen hundred people before a kangaroo court, and shoot them the same night. The verdict was clear before it even came to court. What else happened in La Cabaña? I expect an answer, Che."

"Monique, once we had done away with Batista's savage regime, the people wanted revenge – revenge and yet more revenge. Batista murdered twenty thousand people. But I had to carry out Fidel Castro's orders."

"Che, you're talking like the Nazi bonzes who were condemned at Nuremberg in 1946. They all appealed to the Führer's orders, to orders coming from Adolf Hitler. In my view these big-mouthed lackeys of the Führer were all just cowards."

My brother François – actually he was my half brother, born from my father's first marriage – had been a member of the French Résistance, and fought the Nazis. My father had looked on these activities of his son with a jaundiced eye. My father, together with my Uncle Albert, had owned a small publishing house, and so was obliged from time to time to execute printing orders coming from the Nazi occupation.

François and his small group were fighting the Waffen-SS – the Armed SS. Its members were at the time the most highly trained soldiers in the Second World War. My half brother was audacious and totally fearless, and that was what cost him his life. When attacking a railroad transport, he was wounded and then captured. The Gestapo tortured him to make him reveal the names of his comrades. But he held out, so the Nazis tortured him to death. When he died, he was just nineteen years old. A competitor of my father's told the Nazis that the son of the publisher Cottillard had been a member of the Résistance. He thought he could pick up our small printing business on the cheap. My father and mother were arrested and died on the long journey to a concentration camp in German occupied Poland. I survived only because our neighbor, who was around when they were arrested, told them I was her daughter. I was just an infant in arms. My Uncle Albert and Aunt Claudine escaped to England, taking me with them. There my Uncle Albert, together with General de Gaulle, organized the French resistance movement. Uncle Albert wrote the speeches which de Gaulle broadcast on BBC London. And he also printed the flysheets which were distributed by planes over France by night.

The Allies landed on the Normandy beaches in the summer of 1944, and France was liberated from the Boches. "Boches", pigs – that was what the French called the Germans back then.

I witnessed the return of General de Gaulle to Paris as a child in the arms of my Uncle Albert. People danced with abandon in the streets and squares. They were embracing and singing the Marseillaise.

This liberation was down to the Americans, who now drove in triumph down the Champs-Élysées, enthusiastically applauded by hundreds of thousands of the French.

Uncle Albert got his publishing house back, and also received a great many decorations for his contribution to the resistance. He expanded the firm and started to issue the important political magazine Le Temps.

"You see, Che, we welcomed the Americans," I explained to the revolutionary.

"Monique, I am not proud of what I did at the La Cabaña fortress. Nor am I happy with my job as Minister of Industry, as I am always and everywhere having to make compromises. As a young medical student I worked at a leper colony, I got to know these poor people and grew to be fond of them, even when their face or their whole body was eaten up with the disease. They appreciated me because I treated them like human beings with equal rights. I recognized even back then that the principal reason for their wasting away was not just the disease, but their indescribable poverty. So it became clear to me that a redistribution of the gross national product in South America could only be realized by taking up arms, because the big landowners were not going to give up without a fight."

Che came up very close to me and said, "Monique, one day I will be the greatest revolutionary known to history, greater than Bolívar, Lenin or Mao. One day my name will be known all over the planet. My appearance will be like that of Jesus Christ, and it will be so radiant that everyone else will stand in my shadow."

"Che, you're a megalomaniac! You, Jesus Christ – with a gun in your hand? People like you are filling the lunatic asylums of the whole world, because they fancy that they are Alexander the Great, Napoleon Bonaparte or Jesus Christ!" I yelled at the Minister of Industry, in high rage.

"Monique, why you are you wrecking our time together?"

I thought he was going to hit me – it was well known that South American macho men were given to beating their women on any pretext.

But Che just stroked my cheek and turned in the direction of the door.

"It could have been so beautiful, my little lamb, but I have to go now."

"Just go, Minister, and disappear out of my life! Next time you find yourself rolling around, bleeding and coughing, in a toilet somewhere, just get on the line to your friend Fidel Castro. Let him help you – I am no longer available!"

When Che had gone, I flung myself on the hotel bed and howled like a dog. Gradually I calmed down, and managed to think more reflectively – all through this visit to China, I had been struggling with my emotions. Back in Cuba, Che had a wife and children waiting for him. I had only been an adventure for him – right from the start I had known as much and had actually accepted it. I had no right to dictate any kind of rules to him. Likewise, he had no right at all to pass judgment on my work as a journalist. The Cuban Minister of Industry would have no influence on the tenor of the article I was going to write. Anyway, I wasn't going to have any more meetings with this impertinent goon, I was absolutely sure of that.

Chapter IV

Uncle Albert had very good personal contacts with a lot of ambassadors. He was also well acquainted with the French ambassador to Moscow, Monsieur Marcel Tuffent. The latter had got me a ticket for the famous Bolshoi, as I wanted above all things to see the Bolshoi Ballet perform Tchaikovsky's Swan Lake. Monsieur Tuffent would have been happy to assign me a member of the embassy as a plus one, but I graciously declined this generous offer.

I was utterly thrilled by the music and also by the skills of the ballet troupe. Those Russians showed they had an artistic understanding which must surely be unequaled throughout the world.

When the light came on for the interval, I looked over the railing of my box to see what kind of audience was assembled in this theater. Along with the many Russians in military dress wearing orders and medals, there were also a few soldiers conspicuous in a simple olive green uniform. Suddenly a gaze met me that I would instantly have recognized among thousands. My heart almost stopped; it felt as if a thousand red hot needles were stabbing me in the head. A slight shudder ran down my back, though in the theater it was anything but chilly. *He* had looked up at me. Che too had come to the Bolshoi Theater with his small group of Cubans.

I absolutely did not want to meet this crazy guy again. No doubt he would be imagining that I had come to Moscow in search of him. I stood up, intending to leave the box. But before I could open the door, he was there already and holding me so tightly that it was not possible to get away. With an effort I struggled to get free of his embrace, but he forced me into the corridor.

"Monique, can you forgive me yet again?" were his first words. "Can I visit you? What hotel are you staying in? I'm at the International – it's just behind St. Basil's Cathedral." He talked without giving me a chance to speak.

Privately I had forgiven Che long since, as our confrontation in Beijing had resulted from divergent political opinions in relation to the person of Mao Tsetung. By this time I had checked the information I had obtained in China, with the help of other editors of our journal, and compared it with a variety of other sources. Everything pointed to the fact that the so called "Cultural Revolution" was a gigantic swindle on Mao's part. The official line was that recalcitrant and corrupt party functionaries were being phased out and replaced. This was what Chinese propaganda tried to convince us of. But in reality these party cleansing campaigns were only designed to enable Mao and his wife, Jiang Qing, to hold onto power. Finally Che let me get a word in edgeways. "I've forgotten about that quarrel in Beijing – forgot it a long time ago," I told him. "So I have nothing to forgive you either. My hotel is quite close to the Bolshoi. We can reach it on foot, if you can get away from your delegation."

"For you, Mademoiselle, I would abandon even my own country," he said. This South American macho knew how to compliment a woman. But I liked his easygoing style – actually I had liked it from the very first moment we met.

"I'll let my escorts know that I have to give an important interview, which can only held in privacy," Che said to me.

Soon after we left for my hotel. We had left the theater in the interval, as our recovered intimacy was more important to us than all the ballet music Tchaikovsky ever wrote.

Later on we were lying curled up together in my hotel bed. Che told me why he had been invited to Moscow.

"The Soviet Union has invited all the economics ministers of its sphere of influence to look into the possibilities of increased financial aid for the Third World. My criticism of Russian politics may perhaps after all not have fallen on deaf ears, as it seems that something may finally be moving in the right direction."

"My journal sent me to Moscow for the very same reason – to report directly on the conference of the Comecon states. I wasn't aware that Cuba was a member of Comecon. So I was surprised to find you here in Moscow."

"Actually Cuba is just an associate member of Comecon. I presume that the gentlemen in the Kremlin definitely do want to hear my views about the problem of famine in Third World countries. By the way, of course it makes me happy that your paper should have sent you here of all places, otherwise I wouldn't have met you," Che said with a smile.

The following day we visited Red Square, which had once been a real market place. Against the wall of the

Kremlin, close to the Savior Gate Tower, the Soviets had built Lenin's Mausoleum. Che resolutely made for the queue of persons waiting to get a close view of the founder of the Russian state. "Are there always so many?" I asked Che, as we joined the long queue of Soviet citizens.

"Yes, I've been told that the gigantic numbers of pilgrims haven't let up since Lenin was laid to rest here in his glass coffin." As we entered the dark space of the mausoleum, we saw how people reverentially filed past the man who had called himself Lenin, who now lay in this sarcophagus with a waxen countenance resembling a death mask.

Che, much moved, was ahead of me. He bowed slightly, as he stood right in front of the dead man, and then headed decidedly in the direction of the exit.

Outside in the warm spring sun, the Comandante said to me, "Monique, one day I too will be laid on a bier, and many people, hushed and reverential, will file past me with candles in their hands."

Somewhat surprised, I looked at him, thinking it to be one of his jokes – the kind of joke he had often made in the past – but he meant it in all earnest, indeed in deathly earnest.

Next day Che was waiting for me right after breakfast in the foyer of my hotel. After saying hello, he immediately had a proposal. "Monique, do you fancy going with me to Leningrad? Fidel has asked me to take some pictures of the legendary Winter Palace, which the Bolsheviks stormed in October 1917. Actually the Bolshevik seizure of power took place on 7

November 1917, but as Russia was still following the Julian calendar at the time, the October Revolution was dated to the 25th of October."

Now I remembered those films of the Revolution, "Battleship Potemkin" and "October", which had made Soviet film director Sergei Eisenstein world famous. These silent films had shown the storming of the Winter Palace.

"It would be good for Cuba if the legendary revolutionary Che Guevara could be photographed at this spot," Che explained. "It isn't easy to get a permit to travel from Moscow to Leningrad, but Fidel got it all sorted with Khrushchev some time back by telegram. I'm allowed to be accompanied by a photographer. But my personal preference is for a lady photographic journalist, and I might already have my eye on one I rather like," Che said, and winked at me.

Before the day was out I had received all the necessary documents for our trip to Leningrad. It was extremely difficult for foreigners, even those coming from friendly socialist countries, to travel within the USSR. The Soviet authorities thought every foreigner was an imperialist spy in disguise. If the foreigner then wanted to photograph important buildings, the KGB was convinced that the project must be a threat to national security. Even under the rule of the Tsars, all foreigners had been deeply mistrusted by the authorities.

In view of Fidel Castro's excellent personal contacts with the Supreme Soviet, all the travel permits were handed over to Che by a representative of the Soviet Ministry of the Interior in person. These permits stated that we could move around in Leningrad freely, along with authorization to take photographs of historic buildings. All the buildings were specified by name. Taking photos of military facilities was strictly forbidden. The small package also included two hotel reservations for the Red October hotel in Leningrad.

The train journey was something of an adventure. In the evening a lady ticket collector came and opened out the seats so that they could be used as beds. This hefty female in uniform also handed out the bedding, while all the time keeping several glasses of hot tea balanced on a tray, as she maneuvered through the overcrowded corridor to issue these to the passengers. When boarding the train Che had already tucked a few dollars into her pocket as a tip. No doubt in her eyes it amounted to a small fortune. Now the good woman felt obliged to give us preferential treatment. Not only did she bring us tea every hour, she also regaled us with biscuits, fruit, sticky confectionery and even a plate of borsht – a richly calorific red cabbage soup with added meat. Peasant women came on board at the stations to sell vegetables, eggs and other agricultural products to the passengers.

The powers that be, in the form of police officers and senior railroad employees, turned a blind eye to these transactions. No doubt the odd bottle of vodka or side of bacon had changed hands somewhere along the line. The whole thing pointed to a state of things that I had already come across in a number of socialist countries. This form of barter was also an expression of the economy of scarcity. People were not actually going hungry, and they had reasonably adequate clothing, but still there were long lines forming outside the food stores. When the patient Soviet citizen finally made it to the counter, the piece of meat he was hoping for was often sold out and there was no hope of replenishment.

Early in the afternoon we reached what used to be St. Petersburg. In the First World War it had been known as Petrograd, and now bore the name of Leningrad.

From 1941 to 1944 Leningrad had withstood a blockade lasting almost 900 days, when German army groups surrounded the city. Hundreds of thousands of people died of hunger or cold, as they had no fuel for heating. In view of the famine conditions prevailing, even cases of cannibalism were reported. But the very worst barbarities could not hold back the Red Army, which eventually marched all the way to Berlin.

At the station we took the first taxi that presented itself to our hotel, the Red October. This was situated in the vicinity of the Fourth Winter Palace. I had barely time to pack away my few articles of clothing and toiletries, when Che was knocking on my door, wanting me to accompany him to dinner.

"Wait just a second, I need to freshen myself up. You can help yourself out of the minibar," I called to him. Che clearly had a different idea from mine about "helping himself", as next thing he was standing next to me in the shower stark naked. "If we just freshen up together, that makes it all the more exciting," was all he had to say. Before I could object, his powerful hands had grasped me and pulled me towards him. Fortunately in the USSR many building features were on a much bigger scale than in western European countries. This was certainly the case with the hotel shower, which now had quite a lot to put up with.

Later, with the help of a city map, we worked out the program of activities for the following morning. I checked my photographic equipment, which as a journalist I carried with me wherever I went. Next day we took the taxi that had been put at our disposal for the duration of our stay. Our first port of call was the Fourth Winter Palace.

I showcased Che in his best revolutionary colors. Che in front of the Winter Palace, Che in front of the Peter and Paul Fortress, Che in front of the Menshikov Palace, Che in front of the Academy of Fine Arts, Che in front of the historic Admiralty, which had been planned and built by Andrei Dmitrievich Sakharov in the years from 1805 to 1823.

In all these pictures Che adopted the typical attitude of the revolutionary, with his right hand clenched in a fist. In his other hand he held the inevitable Cuban cigar, which he used as a pointer.

Petersburg natives hurrying past looked somewhat surprised by our activities, but otherwise showed no inordinate interest in the spectacle we put on for them. We were not approached by any of the guardians of public order or other organs of the state. I had however the definite sense that our taxi driver was not just responsible for driving us around in his Moskovich, but was also a member of the Russian secret service, the KGB, closely monitoring our every step and reporting back to his superiors.

Over dinner at our hotel, Che was still excited about the sacred sites of the October Revolution. "Just think, Monique, on 25 October 1917 the Bolshevik troops, along with the worker militias, occupied all the strategic centers in Petrograd. The revolutionary leaders Lenin and Trotsky announced the abdication of Kerenski's bourgeois liberal government, and the councils of workers' and soldiers' delegates, the soviets, came into power.

"On 8 November 1917 the Second All-Russian Congress of Soviets, under Lenin's chairmanship, resolved that the big landowners should be expropriated without compensation. At the same time a decree was passed calling for a general armistice.

"This was the start of the rule of Bolshevism. Russia became the first proletarian global power. Communism was no longer a sect, but a party which kept the entire authority of the state in its own hands.

"A new principle had been thrown out into the world – a revolution that was capable of conquering an empire. Now this fighting spirit was destined to take over the entire world."

I said nothing at the time in response to these high-flown claims by the Cuban Minister of Industry, but deep down I was convinced that the kind of communism currently being practiced here couldn't be the best thing since sliced bread. I didn't want to provoke Che in his flights of fancy, so I kept quiet and enjoyed the fish, and focused on the tones emanating from the piano, where the pianist was giving a rendering of Chopin.

How peaceful the Soviet Union seemed to be! But I knew already, from the reports of Russian dissidents, that the idyll was deceptive. There was seething discontent beneath the surface, and people who disagreed with the regime were getting arrested all the time.

"Monique, tomorrow morning we'll be taking a plane back to Moscow," said Che, interrupting my reflections and pulling me back to reality.

So next day we had to leave Leningrad. I would have liked to spend more time in this Russian Florence, for the city and its people had a special aura for me. Some of aspects of its peculiar charm also reminded me of my own home base, Paris.

The hotel staff gave us an exceptionally friendly send-off, for we had not been stinting with the tips. Western tourists who left a few dollar bills behind them were always welcome, for the American dollar commanded a rate many times higher than the Russian ruble on the black market.

At Moscow airport Che explained to me that for the next two days he was obliged to attend a conference of the Comecon states. He needed to prepare for this important event, as he wanted to report on some of the problems of the Third World. "Tomorrow morning we will be together again, and can spend a few more beautiful days here in the Soviet Union," he told me.

This time frame suited me fine, as I needed to organize my tapes and my written notes. And naturally I wanted to be present at the concluding press conference, to which we had been invited by the Speaker of the Soviet Council of Ministers.

In the following days I heard nothing more about the conference of the Comecon nations. Nor did I hear anything from Che. I asked the reception staff at my hotel if a message had been left for me. I gave the senior reception clerk a few dollars, and asked him to let me know at once if the Cuban Minister of Industry asked after me.

Strangely enough, neither the the television nor the Soviet press agency had any reports about this international conference. On similar past occasions they would always be maundering on, in hackneyed phrases and at inordinate length, about the admirable economic cooperation between the Comecon states.

When I still hadn't heard a word from Che on the day after next, I actually felt a bit queasy. I wondered whether perhaps I should ring the Cuban embassy to inquire about the whereabouts of the Minister of Industry. I rejected the idea at once, because I couldn't think of a plausible reason for wanting to see Che in person. And it couldn't possibly be in his best interests to have western journalists calling his embassy.

Around midday a hotel employee knocked on the door of my suite and handed me a closed unaddressed envelope. When I opened the envelope a card fell into my hands, on which just two lines were written: "Please come at once to my hotel. Don't take a taxi, walk." Although the message bore no signature, it was Che's. I was familiar with his handwriting. Why had he not signed it? What was the meaning of all this hugger-mugger? Had Che locked horns with the KGB? I called the embassy and left a message, telling them about the hotel I was intending to visit. Our embassy was always keen to know in which complex of buildings its journalists were currently to be found. I told them I would be heading for the Hotel International to conduct an interview with the Cuban Minister of Industry.

After a walk of some twenty minutes I reached the hotel, and talked to the reception – who immediately assigned a hotel employee to accompany me. I knocked on the door of Che's suite. Only after repeated knocks did I hear a gasping voice call out, "It's open, come in!" It seemed Che had been expecting me. He was lying in bed and holding a bloody handkerchief to his mouth, coughing into it incessantly. A few used handkerchiefs were lying strewn around the bed.

This reminded me of the similar situation which I had experienced with Che in Algiers.

"At last, my lamb, here you are. I had a bad asthma attack last night. I didn't want to call on the services of a Russian doctor, as I wouldn't be able to trust him."

Later on he told me the whole drama of this supposed Comecon conference. When the Cuban delegation entered the Kremlin conference room, Che was expecting that the economics experts of the numerous Comecon states would be present. But only Russians were in the hall. The chairman was a member of the Presidium of the Supreme Soviet by the name of Brezhnev. He was flanked by two other members of the Supreme Soviet named Kosygin and Podgorny. Apart from this, there were a few Russian economics experts and military bonzes in attendance.

Before Che could start his address – which he had prepared very thoroughly – Brezhnev accused the Cuban of having tried to discredit the glorious Soviet Union all over the world, and so weakening the socialist camp. The imperialist enemy, he said, must be rubbing their hands over his amateurish   utterances. In the Soviet Union this would be regarded as treason and subject to the death penalty. Only in view of his South American origins, and the Soviet Union's cordial friendship with revolutionary Cuba and its leader Fidel Castro, would they refrain from demanding summary punishment.

When Che addressed himself to reply, a Russian economics expert proceeded to list all that Cuba had received from the Soviet Union in material and financial assistance. Without Russian aid, Kosygin asserted, Cuba would have been sunk. The otherwise taciturn Podgorny added his bit by saying, "When a dog bites the hand that feeds him, it's time to have the brute shot!"

Che saw what the Russians were up to. The moment he provided an explanation, a Russian would be trotted out to refute him with economic statistics or some other argument.

This was not an exchange of opinions, it was a tribunal. The Soviets wanted to humiliate and intimidate the revolutionary to such an extent that he would never in future make a public pronouncement criticizing the Soviet Union.

After a while Che had had enough of this theater, and abruptly withdrew, taking his delegation with him.

The Russian contingent looked a bit nonplussed, as no one, in this heartland of the Soviet Socialist Republics, had ever dared do such a thing before.

Che continued his account, still tormented by frequent coughing attacks. "The whole time, I never got to see Khrushchev. I've always had a really good relationship with him. Perhaps if I could have talked to him, the meeting would have taken place in a better atmosphere."

"When I asked where Khrushchev was," Che continued, "the other members of the Presidium exchanged odd looks and gave a disingenuous response. Comrade Khrushchev, they said, was otherwise occupied on important state business. I am even inclined to suspect that a massive power struggle for the top jobs is currently underway at the Kremlin. My request that they should make support of the Third World more of a priority came at a very bad time for these guys, otherwise they wouldn't have reacted so disagreeably!"

I asked Che what he was planning to do. "I must get out of Moscow as soon as possible. It's quite conceivable that this low-down pack of goons might set their sights on me, and try to take me down with an indictment for high treason. Monique, do you think you could pack my things so we can catch the plane tomorrow? I will just have to get back to Fidel Castro with empty hands, which isn't going to do great things for my reputation."

"How about if you put in an intermediate stop in Paris? I could organize meetings with the French Communists and some leftist French intellectuals. Surely a meeting with the philosopher and author Jean-Paul Sartre would be an attractive opportunity for you."

"That's a fabulous idea, Monique. I'm sure Fidel won't complain if I do a bit of publicity for revolutionary Cuba in France. My mother Celia de la Serna, who came from one of the most highly regarded families of Argentina, always saw Paris as being the archetype of beauty and culture. She introduced me to the French language as well." Che already seemed to have cheered up – it was always astonishing how quickly he recovered from his asthma attacks. But another thought was still going through my head. Could Fidel Castro have deliberately and intentionally thrown Che to the Moscow wolf pack, to prevent him discrediting the Kremlin bosses in future?

Chapter V

Uncle Albert was completely over the moon. "Monique, however did you manage to lure the Cuban Minister of Industry to Paris?" I was sitting with him in his office at the publishing house, to give him an immediate report, on my return from Moscow, about the Comecon conference that had not taken place, and Che's personal disaster.

In conclusion I said to my uncle: "There can be no doubt that a change of power in the Soviet Union is imminent. There wasn't a word about this conference in the media. Khrushchev has not appeared in public for some while. Che's visit to Moscow came at the worst possible time."

Uncle Albert showed me the latest editions of the French dailies, all of them carrying accounts of Che's arrival at Paris's Orly airport, and his triumphal parade through the city in an open car. In front of the classy Hotel Ritz where he was staying, the hotel staff had formed up in two lines as a guard of honor for their distinguished Cuban guest.

"All this trouble, when he isn't even an official representative on a state visit! Monique, you must stick to the revolutionary for all you're worth, we're going to give him prime time coverage on this visit to Paris. It looks as if you've got a hot line to the man. I'll just make a few essential phone calls, to ensure he gets introduced to the right people. Then you can have a lengthy exclusive interview printed in Le Temps."

"Uncle, we need to take care that we don't try to

commandeer him – he can be quite touchy. Let me talk to him first, to find out who he would like to see and which busybodies he would prefer to avoid."

"But of course! It goes without saying that we can get things clear with him in advance, as far as possible. You do seem to be on very personal terms with him. Are we looking at something more here than a relationship between interviewer and interviewee?" asked the elderly gentleman, who certainly gave no sign of senility.

Under his scrutiny, I blushed to the roots of my hair.

"I suspected as much, as your photos in Leningrad were fantastic, but they did also indicate that there was an intimate relationship between the photographer and the subject. Monique, you are a grown person, you can and indeed must follow your own path – but I wouldn't like to see you made unhappy," Uncle Albert said in concerned tones.

"You are and always will be my very best uncle in the whole wide world," I said, and fell upon his neck.

I got on the line to the Hotel Ritz and asked politely to speak to the Cuban Minister of Industry. In a short time Che was on the phone. He too seemed in high spirits about his reception. "The atmosphere here is quite fabulous. My mother was right about Paris when she said it had something special."

"Che, could you please come to Montmartre, and wait for me outside the Basilica of the Sacré-Cœur? I want to show you a bit of Paris. Along the way we can discuss what people you want to make contact with while you are here. Montmartre is swarming with tourists from all over the world, so we won't be too conspicuous. Please wear something to make you look like a regular traveler – it would be most unpleasant if a pack of paparazzi attached themselves to our heels."

At the Sacré-Cœur there were plenty of tourists milling about, but Che was nowhere to be seen. Finally a middle aged man spoke to me, asking if I could tell him how to get to the Louvre. I pulled out a map of Paris and gave the friendly gentleman a detailed explanation of how to reach the world famous museum.

"Actually I don't want to visit a museum, I'd prefer a pleasure palace of Louis XIV. Would you do me the honor of accompanying me there, Mademoiselle Cottillard?" he asked, outrageously. Now I recognized the middle aged man. He had a bald head, and was very much altered in other respects – but it was Che! He had clearly been well worked over by a makeup artiste.

"The head porter at the Ritz put me in touch with this very talented lady, when I told him I was concerned not to be recognized."

"Yes, let's go to Versailles – it's a place where French and European history was made."

We both laughed over this mummery, and I agreed to Che's suggestion that we should visit the famous palace. "First we go to the nearest Metro station, then we take the Paris subway and carry on by bus to reach Versailles", I explained to my companion.

At the entrance to the Versailles park a tramp was sitting with a baguette in his hand, while with his other hand he raised a small piece of Camembert to his mouth. Evidently we were looking at the King of the

Tramps, for the man was tall and fat, with a wild red shock of hair which merged with a dense red beard. In what was left of his face an oversized nose stood out, which showed all the colors of the rainbow. His tattered clothing and perforated shoes were covered all over with streaks of grime.

The beggar gave no impression of humility, sitting in majesty on his bench as if he thought the world belonged to him. I rushed up to Che to say that he shouldn't stare at the man in this way, as his interest might be misinterpreted and could lead to a confrontation.

The tramp paid no attention to Che at all, looking just at me. He raised his hand, executed an elegant hand movement with the suggestion of a bow, as if he were at the court of Louis Quatorze, and said, "*Enfin j'ai rendez-vous avec un rayon de soleil*" – "Finally I meet up with a ray of sunshine." Che laughed so heartily and with such abandon that I could not help joining in. The man sitting there, in his torn coat stiff with dirt, was telling me that he was meeting a ray of sunshine, and the ray of sunshine was presumably me. Che gave the man a franc bill, which disappeared very quickly into some inner pocket of his coat. But he didn't want our charity; he invited us to dine with him. He broke off a piece of his baguette for each of us and placed a bit of soft cheese on the bread. Overcoming some strong inner resistance, I ate the meal I was offered. Che seemed not to be bothered at all, for he even drank a sip of red wine from the fat-bellied bottle the tramp held out to him.

The King of the Beggars seemed to be of a philo-sophical bent, as he was ready and willing to tell us his philosophy of life. "I've completely given up material things, which are supposed to make our lives richer and better. Since then I've been free of all compulsions, and have been able to enjoy my new life to the full. Be-hold the birds in the field and in the air! They sow not neither do they reap, and yet they live, says the Lord. The park, the flowers, the trees and animals living here all belong to me. So do the sculptures and the pictures in the museums. To me belongs the jewelry you see in the jewelers' windows, for I can look at it any time I like. If someone purchases a valuable brooch, all he can do is look at it, and see the precious stones gleam and sparkle in the sun." Che laughed heartily again at the tramp philosopher, and handed him another franc bill, which he didn't want to accept. "*Non, non, Monsieur!* You offend me, because I invited you to share some of my food with me," the man insisted. Che looked at him for a long time, and finally said: "Just take it, Monsieur Philosopher, and when you drink a drop of red wine with your friends, raise your glass to Comandante Che, who you once invited to share a meal. One day I will look just like you, only the beauties of nature will then be a closed book to me, because my eyes will be bro-ken and fixed and staring at the sky."

Again I was surprised that Che could say such a thing. He pronounced the words with such seriousness that the tramp stared at him with a shocked expression.

At the portal leading to the park I purchased two tick-ets entitling us to visit the palaces. First we proceeded through the Grand Trianon, which was being traversed by a group of American tourists at the same time. Finally we wanted to visit the Petit Trianon as well, but the attendant told us that no more guided tours would be taking place that day.

For a certain deposit, however, he would let us have the keys to the royal apartments. I had spontaneously declared that I could do the guiding myself, as I had been here many times before.

"Are you aware, I asked Che, "what these buildings were used for?"

"Servants' quarters, perhaps," observed the Comandante.

"Yes, servants in a sense – but actually it was the ladies of the night, the favorites of the kings, who were housed here," I explained. At the back of the building was a room containing exceptionally fine Rococo furniture and crystal chandeliers. We were completely alone in the palace, enveloped in a wonderful stillness.

"So this was where those absolutist rulers lived and loved, before the great revolution put an end to their fun and games," Che said.

"Yes," I put in – "later on the king was no longer the complete article, because the Jacobins made him shorter by a head."

"Look, Monique, I seem still to be in possession of all my bodily parts. We can play kings and mistresses." He had already picked me up and carried me to the gigantic four poster bed, which was surrounded on all sides with silken curtains.

"Che, not here for God's sake! What if someone comes in!"

"I locked the main gate, and the key is still safely stowed in my pocket."

The absolute ruler had assembled all his playmates around him; now he chose his favorite of the day. His choice fell on me. The lackeys led me into the Petit Trianon, which was festively decorated with all the flowers of the spring. The light of many hundred candles was reflected back from the crystal mirrors, to illuminate the majestic room with vastly amplified illumination. I floated as if on wings. When I woke up, it was not a French king lying beside me but my beloved Che. I hadn't been sharing a bed with some Louis the Umpteenth, but with him – and that was just what I wanted.

"You fell asleep straight away, and I was the same," the Cuban explained.

"One sleeps exceptionally well in the four poster bed of the king's mistress," I commented, still a bit sleepy.

"These public nuisances, or rather parasites, who lived high on the hog at the cost of the starving population, certainly knew how to enjoy the pleasures of life," said the revolutionary.

"Absolutism was just one epoch of history – after the Revolution, that is to say after the Reign of Terror of the Jacobins and the megalomania of Napoleon Bonaparte, a great period of reflection dawned for European philosophers. A phase of inner and outer liberation, and humanism, inspired great numbers of poets and thinkers in the nineteenth century," I said, in an endeavor to make sense of it all.

"I think the idea of humanism is a will o' the wisp. There is no such thing as humanity developing into an improved version, that is, into a humanist human being," Che stated.

"How can you say such a thing? – you as a convinced Communist," I riposted, rather violently.

"That's just the way it is, unfortunately. Anyone who wants to make radical changes to the world is embarked on a dangerous course. He runs the risk of terrorizing his environment or perhaps even a whole people – even if he pursues his struggle in the name of humanity. This was the case with the Jacobins, with the Bolsheviks under Lenin, and under Stalin government repression reached immeasurable proportions."

"Child labor and slavery were done away with, women were given the vote, torture and wars of aggression were banned," I countered.

"All these so called human rights can be canceled overnight, just at a stroke," Che remarked.

"That means that according to your view of history the western democracies could reintroduce torture and concentration camps?"

"Doubtless the USA would set up concentration camps if it felt itself under threat – and your fatherland, my dear Monique, practiced torture wholesale during the Algerian war."

"But humanist values are still with us – like human rights for instance. This ideal is indestructible, surely you must see that!"

"Human beings are not just *eros*, they are *thanatos*

as well – with a tendency towards aggression, cruelty and the lust to destroy. That is why any progress is double-edged. The increase of knowledge makes people more powerful, both for good things and for bad. This is true in relation to nature as well as in relation to other human beings. *Homo sapiens* is at the same time *Homo rapiens*, a predator with monstrous destructive power, capable of plunging the world into the abyss."

Che seemed to think that put an end to the discussion, which had been carried on in the lavish bed of the mistresses of Louis XIV. As so often, I tried to have the last word.

"You can escape into your end of the world fantasies if you want. But as a journalist, I will always defend human rights, and that means giving my total and unreserved support to all emancipatory efforts of oppressed peoples."

"I'm not surrendering to unworldly fantasies, far from it. I will be at the forefront of all freedom movements all over the world, and carry on the struggle until the point where a bullet terminates my existence."

Again Che pronounced these weighty words as if he were talking about the fine points of yesterday's dinner. Quite unexpectedly, a hand pulled back the curtain of our royal four poster bed, and a somewhat agitated voice addressed us: "How dare you pollute this historic piece of furniture with your orgies?" It was the palace gatekeeper standing there before us, his face a study in indignation.

I disappeared at once under the coverlet, intending not to re-emerge in the foreseeable future.

"Oh, I am so sorry, Monsieur, we have been in a terrible situation. The husband of Madame here has been stalking her for days with his jealousy, he threatens her and beats her, but the poor lady doesn't want to go back to this villain. And besides he is searching through all the hotels and pensions in Paris to find where Madame might be staying. We took refuge in this place only because we were practically desperate. I beg you, kind sir, don't report us to the authorities!"

Che's voice sounded so tearful, that even the marble busts in this royal salon seemed liable to burst into tears out of pure sympathetic emotion.

The gatekeeper was of course a real Frenchman, who understood about situations like this. A generous tip, which Che passed to the good man, put him in a somewhat better humor.

After getting back to my office, I made a few telephone calls to arrange a date between Che and the Chairman of the French Socialists. I also contacted the First Secretary of the Communist Party of France to get him to agree to a meeting with Che Guevara.

For almost two days I heard practically nothing from Che. I knew, however, that he had conducted some important meetings in the mean time, the results of which he wanted to relay to Cuba.

Suddenly on the Sunday morning came a call from the Hotel Ritz. Che asked if we could meet in his suite. When I entered Che's room and he greeted me, as ever, with a kiss on the cheek, I sensed at once that he was very cast down.

I soon learned the reasons for his depression. Neither Viktor Duris, the Chairman of the Socialists, nor Fabris Tirard, the First Secretary of the Communist Party, had been able to summon up the least bit of enthusiasm for the requests of the Cuban Minister of Industry. They made no apologies in the matter of development assistance for Cuba, nor were they willing to support freedom movements in Africa or South America. Che saw Duris as being a Frenchman still caught up in the toils of colonialist thinking, while Tirard had branded him as a person fouling his own nest, and bringing discredit on the international Communist movement.

So Che had made no progress whatsoever with his project of advancing the liberation of the Third World.

"Nothing but ignorant groveling sneaks," the revolutionary complained, heaping further choice epithets of Spanish origin on the men he had been talking to.

Before he could get even more worked up with his South American temperament, I asked him how he wanted to proceed from here.

"I've had a telegram from Fidel telling me to get back to Cuba as soon as possible. At five tomorrow morning my flight leaves for Havana," Che told me.

"Oh dear, so we've only got one day left – who knows when we are going to meet again," I said, disappointed.

"Monique," said Che, pressing himself against me, "the night is ours as well – and even if they should turn out to be the last hours we spend on earth together, we will make the most of them."

Chapter VI

In the following week I had an interview with historian of economics Roger Dilhaud.

"Monsieur Dilhaud, is there a real alternative to the capitalist system?" was my first question.

"Mademoiselle Cottillard, I can tell you quite definitely that there are no viable alternatives to capitalism in evidence."

"The free market economy is repeatedly shaken by crises, what can we do to prevent this?"

"The citizens and the electorate must recognize that crises are endemic to this system, because it just is a risky social structure, one in which there will always be winners and losers. Many speculators in the banking sector have got their noses in the trough, and this means that they are frequently unscrupulous and dishonest. The risk that they will ever be brought to book for their dishonest dealings is minimal, as in the case of greater losses the tax payer would have to foot the bill.

"Nationalization of the banks, and also of key industries, would be one possible solution. But state bureaucracies, as in the so called people's democracies, would not be the answer. Training managers to conduct their business in such a way that it is to the benefit of all, rather than raking in short term profits, would undoubtedly make more sense.

"The next reshaping of society must not be brought about at the barricades with machine guns, but should be conducted peacefully and democratically. Freely elected parliaments must expel the profiteers. A wealth tax and VAT on stock market dealings might draw some of the venom from unbridled capitalism. So I repeat – there is no other sociopolitical system that works any more efficiently than capitalism does."

After we had exchanged a few more private opinions on general matters, I left the financial expert in a somewhat thoughtful mood. Did this mean Che Guevara's way was completely wrong, perhaps it was even just an anachronism?

Whereas we young people in Paris had always been raised in a rather looser and more liberal way, those in the provinces were constantly subject to the strict regime of the Catholic church. This applied to French girls particularly.

From the mid-fifties on, the rock 'n' roll wave flooded over to Europe from the USA.

A young singer by the name of Elvis Presley, who coaxed a very special rhythm out of his guitar, became the idol of an entire generation.

French singers and songstresses copied the music of the Americans, to the disapproval of the older generation. Teenagers started to rebel all over Europe. The rock 'n' roll star Johnny Hallyday was adored by the French youth, while older adults took a severe dislike to him.

The music of the rock 'n roll era was not just a nine days wonder – it kept going for a good few years before being replaced by the beat wave of the Beatles and the Rolling Stones. Along with their music, young people finally developed their own fashions, their new easygoing modes of social intercourse and to cap it all, a new critical attitude to all former conventions of the adult world. It was a declaration of war against the restoration spirit of the Charles de Gaulle and Konrad Adenauer era.

Our weekly had given me the job of writing a report about the revolution of the Sixties. I traveled the provinces and interviewed mayors, priests, academics and young people on the subject of the new youth culture. Whereas the older generation took an extremely critical view of young people, many of them even calling for firm repressive measures, some sociologists and political thinkers had a more open-minded view of the phenomenon.

I interviewed the well-known biologist Professor Gilbert Cantet. His views were these: "The English scientist Charles Darwin made a discovery in the nineteenth century which large numbers of church members, as well as other sectors of the population, have been totally unwilling to accept up to the present day. In the American provinces teachers are still being threatened by parents for passing on Darwin's teachings – the theory of evolution, that is – to their students."

"What does the theory of evolution state?" I asked the professor.

"These discoveries, Mademoiselle, were based on evidence Darwin had collected in the course of his voyages in many different parts of the world. The diversity of the animal kingdom as, he encountered it on the Galapagos Islands, made a particular impression on him.

"Human beings – this was the conclusion of Darwin's

many years of research – had developed from single cell to multicellular organisms, eventually evolving into a living being, a mammal, that was the primeval father or mother of anthropoid apes and human beings."

"But *Monsieur le Professeur*, there was no way the Christian churches were going to accept this," I interpolated.

"You're completely right. When Darwin published his findings, there were violent protests, and not just from the ranks of the church; some scientists as well broke off all contacts with Darwin. Even death threats were made against the scholar, who had been working in his laboratory in what would today be seen as primitive conditions. He had brought many thousand specimens home from overseas, in order to experiment with the collected samples.

"Darwin's findings have now been confirmed worldwide by scientists, who conduct their research today with increasingly elaborate equipment, ranging as far as atomic force microscopy.

"But the theory of evolution also states that this process of development has not been completed to the present day. The entire plant and animal kingdoms are thus engaged in an ongoing process of transformation. And the same is true of human beings."

"So you are saying, *Monsieur le Professeur*, if I understand you correctly, that human beings have been and continue to be shaped by their environment?"

"But of course, Mademoiselle Cottillard. Taken all in all, nature is enormously adaptable, and one part of it is the human being. Human beings survived the Ice

Age, all the following climatic changes, all the wars we have had to date, including the dropping of the first atomic bomb. Nature is very inventive when it is a matter of survival. But that also means that one day humanity will have come to the end of the road."

"What kind of thing might put a period to human existence?" I asked the distinguished academic.

"There could be many causes. First of all natural catastrophes, like impacting meteors or epidemics – possibly climatic changes as well, which could cause the sea level to rise all over the world. Human aberrations, it goes without saying, could be an equally significant factor."

"You mean world wars, where the use of weapons of mass destruction could spell the end of humanity," I put in.

"Yes, that is undoubtedly right, but in the past it wasn't just wars which resulted in the collapse of empires. A considerable degree of decadence was often found as well, as a factor leading humanity into the abyss. Once upon a time, people made rules for themselves: first of all as rituals to strengthen the sense of community, and then to soothe their fear of death – something from which no one is immune. People were told that death is not the end, that they would go on living after they were dead. In this way much of the terror was taken out of death, and it became possible to mobilize the population for certain objects. People were obliged to bear arms or wear uniform, and might have to go to war in case of need."

"Who was responsible for all this manipulation?"

"Of course it was the authorities, as well as the church with whom they were in league. The princes, kings and emperors ruled by the grace of God and so were unassailable, as the church taught. Even in pre-Christian times, certain burial rituals had a crucial part to play. I would just like to remind you of the Egyptian pyramids, or the Mayan ones in Central America. The idea was to alleviate people's fear of an unknown form of existence into which they enter when they die."

"What is your own personal view of the idea of 'life after death'?" I asked.

"Mademoiselle Cottillard, I am afraid I must disappoint you. No doubt you expect me to confirm the theses of religion stating that human beings continue to exist in some form or other – whether in heaven or in hell, or at least in a beast, as some Asian religions inform us. But I cannot confirm this, as I have never met a human being from another dimension. I see just an outside possibility, in that at some distant time our entire galaxy could collide with another Milky Way, both systems would melt together, and this would give rise to new life once more. As is well known, the massive meteor bombardments which afflicted our earth first of all destroyed large parts of the life existing on the planet, but later gave rise to new life in a more highly developed form."

"Is there no almighty power in existence, controlling the microcosm as well as the macrocosm? Or to put it more simply – does God exist?"

"I knew you would be coming to this question before long. I do often get asked about the existence of God.

God exists in the form of our intelligence and through our conscience. I just can't picture him as a great creator and switchman.

"Trillions of years ago our universe was just a gigantic empty space. A nothing, as it were. Things remained this way for a few billion years, seeing that nature of course has infinite time for development. One day a massive explosion occurred, from which all galaxies and stars later came into being. This Big Bang, so called, has continued until the present day, with new heavenly bodies constantly being created while others come to an end.

"As you can see from this, the originally empty space was not so empty after all, for minute particles, smaller than an atom, hurtled around in this gigantic arena at immense speed. After billions of years the critical particles collided and so released the Big Bang. The gas clouds that came into being compacted, first into gaseous bodies, like our sun, and then forming solid bodies like our earth.

"I am often told, in response to my earlier observations, that in that case there must exist an all-embracing power, to have scattered the minute particles through the void in the first place. I'm afraid I can't confirm that, but I can't refute it either. At all events it would make sense not to wait for trillions of years before creating life in the image of God. And why the wastage of creating so many planets inimical to life? I am firmly convinced that life does exist on other planets. But for human life to evolve, many favorable factors must be present simultaneously. I repeat once again, everything that human beings have thought with reference to a higher power has served in the last resort only for the survival of the species.

"There is a divine force in us, given to us by nature: our intelligence and our conscience. As for the descriptions in the Bible which speak of a God or the Son of God, who died for the redemption of humanity, I would assign them to the realm of legend. The churches need these legends to strengthen their power, or as in earlier centuries to keep the poor folk under their thumb. I hope this answers your question about the existence of God, Mademoiselle Cottillard."

I thanked him for the interview, and took my leave of the famous scientist.

Uncle Albert had contacted the Dalai Lama's secretary to arrange a meeting for me with the God-King of Tibet, now living in exile. I met the global supreme head of Tibetan Buddhism in a separate meeting room of the Savoy Hotel.

"Your Holiness, where do you live when you are not traveling?" I asked at the outset of the interview with the supreme spiritual dignitary of the Tibetans.

"Since I fled my own country I have been living in Dharamsala in India, and I am very grateful to the Indian government for giving me a home. It is the country of Mahatma Gandhi, whose mighty resistance to English colonial power makes him something of a role model for me."

"The supreme head of the Catholic church, the Pope, claims to be infallible. Does this also apply to the Dalai Lama?" was my next question.

"That I can definitely answer in the negative. My teaching is based on tolerance and goodwill toward my fellow human beings. I am in touch with representatives of governments all over the world, with the aim of regaining independence and autonomy for Tibet. But I want this to happen in a peaceful way."

"It doesn't look as if China is going to pay much attention to any kind of appeal by the United Nations," I commented. "They are more likely to send even more forces of occupation to nip any resistance brutally in the bud."

"Yes, there has been so much suffering, so much despair to date. I am just very sad, deeply sad. If I ever harbor thoughts of ill will against those who are now in power, I practice meditation in order to overcome all negative emotions and recover my equilibrium. Our faith says that even when you receive hate from your enemies, you should broadcast compassion back. So I pray for the dead and the wounded, whether they are Tibetan or Chinese."

"Your Holiness, Tibet was a feudal empire where powerful monasteries engaged in bloody struggles. Some Dalai Lamas did not die in their beds but were murdered."

"Mademoiselle, that is so. As a result of the deep devotion of the Tibetans to Buddhism, blatant injustices came about, as some vainglorious abbots became addicted to the pursuit of power. As you know, I tried to introduce democratic institutions to my homeland. And I did succeed in pressing through some reforms. But then the invasion of the Communists put a stop to all my efforts."

"What is special about the myth of Tibet?" I asked the god-king.

"There are a great many people in this world who are looking for the meaning of life. My country is a rugged mountainous country with many snow-covered eight thousand meter peaks. You can call it the roof of the world. Because of its turquoise lakes and peaceful atmosphere, many people believe this is the real paradise, where you might be able to find peace. Sadly this is not the case, as you can see from what has befallen my countrymen and myself."

"Do you think, your Holiness, that any improvement of the situation in the next years can be expected?"

"The Chinese have a massive economic interest in Tibet. Our country is rich in minerals. The Chinese want to exploit its resources, so they are not going to relinquish control of Tibet for a long time. As a result, I don't believe in a rapid solution of the Tibetan question. My prayers continue to be offered on behalf of all the people of this earth." With these words, the fourteenth Dalai Lama took his leave of me.

His secretary accompanied me to a sliding door in the next room, where he bowed many times and wished me all the best for the future.

Chapter VII

The plenary hall of the UNO's main building was occupied down to the last seat. The journalists thronging the press galleries waited with bated breath for the entry of the Cuban Minister of Industry, Ernesto "Che" Guevara.

Some days earlier Che had sent me a telex message, asking me to come to New York to hear his speech in the UNO plenary assembly. The real reason for our coming together, however, was a meeting which could be of crucial importance for his political future.

The message had reached me in encrypted form. The letters had been replaced with numbers, in such a way that the text could not be decrypted by simple methods. The first letter was not a 1 – it might just as well be a 542, for example. Only a secret services specialist would have been able to decipher the script. Che had explained to me how it worked when he was staying in Paris, and taught me how to use the key which he had devised himself.

I informed Uncle Albert of my imminent trip to New York to attend the plenary assembly of the UN, following which I should be getting an exclusive interview with the Cuban Minister of Industry.

"Monique, you can't be expecting to meet up with him again at the first opportunity. I just hope you won't have any kind of difficulty with the secret services. Diplomatic complications between France and the United States, such as might arise from a love affair between a minister and a lady journalist, would be extremely damaging to the serious reputation of our weekly. This Che Guevara is no doubt an unbelievably well educated person, but at the same time he is a ticking time bomb, liable to explode at any moment. I am concerned that you might vanish at short notice into the jungle of the secret services. Of course you are full grown, but I do still feel a certain sense of responsibility, because your parents made me promise to look after you."

My uncle looked at me with his kindly brown eyes full of concern. I felt again like the ten year old girl of the old days, when I used to play some crazy pranks with the boy next door. Once we jumped down from the highest beam of the barn ceiling, onto a pile of freshly mown hay that was stored there. Unfortunately a wooden strut got in the way and interrupted my acrobatic interlude. I broke my left arm. Now my uncle was looking at me in the very same way as back then – as if the same thing was liable to happen.

"Dear Uncle Albert, I promise you I won't do anything that would put our country or our journal at risk."

I gave him a kiss on the cheek, after which he seemed to take a somewhat more positive view of the world.

"Monique, I know your character and what genes you have inherited. I will go on trusting you, now and in future." On that note he said goodbye, just before I left for New York.

For all those journalists not already familiar with the United Nations Organization, guided tours were offered with the object of publicizing the multifarious tasks of the institution. We were also shown all the premises not subject to conditions of secrecy.

Our guide, a female member of staff, showered the group with facts and figures. The UNO was founded by fifty-one nations in San Francisco on 26 June 1945, as a successor organization to the League of Nations. Today the UN had a hundred and sixty-three members, with new ones being added all the time. Its principal headquarters were in New York, with a European representative office in Geneva. The plenary assembly of all members was held at least once a year. It debated all topical issues that came under the charter of the organization. Consultations on important problems – maintaining peace and security, for instance, or the co-option or expulsion of members – called for a two thirds majority; in connection with other questions, a simple majority was sufficient.

"The United Nations Security Council," she went on, "consists of five permanent members: the USA, the Soviet Union, Great Britain, France, the People's Republic of China, along with ten more alternating members. It carries the principal responsibility for the introduction and execution of procedures for the peaceful settlement of international conflicts. According to the organization's charter, the members are obliged to follow its decisions. Every member of the Council has one vote; any permanent member can in addition impose a veto to block any decision of the Council.

"The International Court of Justice in the Hague is the successor to the Permanent Court of International Justice of the League of Nations. Only states can appeal to it. It consists of fifteen judges who are elected by the Plenary Assembly and the Security Council.

"The Economics and Social Council, consisting of fifty-four members, fosters economic and social development and peaceful cooperation between nations on all levels, and tries to enforce generally accepted human rights all over the world."

The explanations of the UN guide were a bit too long-winded for me. I could find out about what went on at the UN by looking at one of the prospectuses laid out all round the building. For that reason, I left the UN headquarters.

I had found accommodation at the Hotel Waldorf Astoria. Luckily I was able to reach Che at his hotel. He gave me to understand that we could not possibly meet at his hotel, as it was swarming with secret agents of all colors. The Comandante would be visiting me under the name of Ramón Benitez Fernández, a businessman of Uruguayan origin. I had no way of knowing at this point that he would use this name later on to enter Bolivia, with the aim of starting his Bolivian revolution.

On the morning of the same day Che appeared to me in a completely altered guise. He looked a bit the way he had done back in Paris, but this time he was even more radically transformed, so that even his nearest and dearest would not have recognized him. The Minister of Industry had a half bald head, and he was wearing glasses and a cheekpiece. All the secret agents walked right past him, none of them aware that Che Guevara was concealed behind this mask.

His voice, his movements and his hands, which once again were stroking me repeatedly, however left me in no doubt however that I was holding my beloved in my arms once more.

Che made a rather restless impression. He kept coughing, and had to inhale over and over again. His power of attraction and his erotic aura, which made me like putty in his hands, had however not deserted him. The modest lunch he had ordered for us would have to wait, the revolutionary stated. At the moment he didn't have any appetite for this kind of pleasure, though he was more than capable of getting excited about other beautiful aspects of life.

Was it the firm hold of his hands, or was it the rhythm of the Argentinian tango that I seemed to sense in his every touch? Che always took me to unimaginable heights – higher than the highest peaks of the Andes.

Later we lay exhausted alongside in my hotel bed. He told me about his work, and was very critical of his own performance. Originally he had seen his job as Cuban Minister of Industry as a vocation, but now he hated it.

"Monique, I wanted to bring about radical economic changes in Cuba. The abolition of private property in relation to all the means of production was meant to be the trademark of the Cuban revolution, indeed to serve as a model for the whole of South America. The land reform we initiated was bound to lead to confrontation with the United States. Step by step I nationalized the landholdings of the banks, of industry and foreign trade. The US then imposed a trade embargo on Cuba. Under pressure from the American imperialists, the other countries of Central and South America were forced to boycott us as well. With great difficulty I managed to persuade some states, socialist states above all, to resume buying sugarcane from us. At the same time I was carrying out intensive industrialization, so as to reduce our dependence on sugarcane exports.

"A succession of poor harvests, mistakes in the course of industrialization, constant secret intrigues within the ruling Unity Party and growing bureaucratization all led to an economic disaster and to an ever growing dependency on the Soviet Union.

"The so called Cuban missile crisis made me realize with terrible clarity that our little country is only a football for the two global powers. Our country is plunged into a deep economic crisis, for which I have to admit responsibility.

"Monique, I have failed!

"This bureaucratic fiddling with figures, these back-stabbing intrigues, they aren't really my thing. All I need is a few devoted comrades to fight against exploitation and in a righteous cause. Really, I am just born to be a revolutionary."

"In what country do you think to take up the revolutionary struggle?" I asked the Comandante.

"Revolutionary China and its great Communist leader Mao Tse-tung have got their eye on the dark continent, on Africa. That is where I will carry on the struggle against imperialism and neocolonialism."

"Why don't you export the Cuban revolution to South

America? Surely that would be the obvious course," I observed.

"Monique, of course I am very much interested in Latin America, but it is a long and difficult battle. Our policy of taking the revolution from country to country in South America has proved abortive.

"Recently a close friend of mine was killed – my comrade Jorge Ricardo Masetti, who commanded a partisan group and was fighting the Argentinian military.

"All our activities of this kind in South America to date have been a mistake. I bear the responsibility for these defeats."

On the following day I listened with bated breath to the Cuban Minister of Industry's address to the UNO plenary assembly. His speech however did not include anything new that pointed to the future. Che again repeated his attacks on US imperialism and on the socialist countries, who in their trade relations with the Third World were only interested in their own advantage, and so could be seen as accomplices of the imperialists. His literal words were: "As Marxists we remain convinced that peaceful co-existence between nations does not imply co-existence between exploiters and the exploited, between the oppressors and the oppressed." Later on he continued: "The Cuban revolutionaries have the moral obligation to spread the ideological flame of the revolution all over America and to all the countries of the world. Wherever people listen to us, we have the obligation to raise people's awareness of misery, exploitation and injustice – the obligation that José Martí summed up in an utterance we should always keep in mind. He said that every real human being must feel the blow on his own shoulder that any other human being is dealt. That must be the revolutionary attitude to all the peoples of the world."

After this UNO appearance of the Minister of Industry, I had no contact with Che for three days. He had however indicated at our last meeting that he might be getting in touch with a close confidant of the American President. It was essential to keep this meeting secret.

Che then came to see me at my suite in the Waldorf Astoria. Although he tried to appear cheerful and relaxed, I immediately noticed that in reality he was very cast down.

"I had a lengthy talk with a certain Minister Zuckerman, who has a direct line to the American President. My offer to the USA was very generous. We would pay appropriate compensation to all American landholders in Cuba, the sugarcane plantations and the processing plants. I was even prepared to desist from all revolutionary activities currently being exported from Cuba to other countries, if the USA would lift the trade embargo and recognize Cuba as a socialist state.

"Zuckerman gave no assurances, but promised me he would present this offer to his President. That very moment, Monique, it became crystal clear to me that there is no possibility of a modus vivendi between us and the United States of America."

In the course of giving this account, Che had been coughing so badly that he was hardly able to speak.

When he coughed into his handkerchief yet again, I saw that it was getting increasingly red, which might indicate the imminence of a hemorrhage. I let him lean on me as I helped him to the bathroom. Fortunately he had his inhaler with him, so the affliction soon subsided. We sat for some time in close embrace on the couch, watching the glowing red sun sink over the concrete canyons of Manhattan.

"Monique, I'm going to submit my resignation as Minister of Industry and go back to being a revolutionary. Everything I have told you today must be kept strictly under wraps. One day I will contact you again."

Chapter VIII

In the hospital tent, the wounded men were screaming in pain. "Doctor Comandante, we desperately need blood plasma and painkillers," the colored nurse begged the Cuban. "Could you please drive over to Colonel Sambe and get medical supplies."

Che, who was himself not in very good shape, as he was suffering constant asthma attacks, leaped into the jeep they had liberated from the enemy to drive to Brazzaville. He looked for his traveling companions, Comrades Pombo and Bramlio, to get them to go with him. He finally found them surrounded by a crowd of naked children who were larking with the Cubans. Che needed Comrade Pombo as a bodyguard, as the few viable roads were constantly watched by Tschombe's soldiers. Comrade Bramlio was needed as an interpreter, so he could converse with Sambe.

The Colonel was a former tribal chief, to whom the socialist revolution of the Republic of Brazzaville meant something as long as he received material aid from the countries of the eastern bloc. This aid – in the form of all kinds of supplies, weapons, food and medicines – he distributed first of all to his family clan, and then to the people. If one day this aid were to be discontinued, he would be the first to fight on the opposite side for Tschombe's Republic of the Congo. Che had long since come to curse the day when he and his one hundred and twenty-five well armed guerillas had first set foot on African soil.

The wind of travel made Che's mane of hair fly in the breeze, so that his famous beret was blown off his head. Half way to their destination, Che suddenly heard an engine noise that drowned out the noise of their own jeep. With a quick turn of the steering wheel to the right, Che drove the jeep into a clump of trees where the low hanging foliage gave them some cover.

But before the vehicle came to a stop, Che and his companions hurled themselves out of it and dropped to the floor of the dusty savanna – just in time, for the jeep had been hit by an explosive missile. The parts of the vehicle flew through the air, narrowly missing the guerilleros. The combat helicopter flew over the place where Che and his comrades were hiding a few more times, and a few rounds were fired from a machine gun, but none found their mark.

The noise of the rotors receded slowly, until finally it died away altogether. Che, Pombo and Bramlio crawled out of the hollow where they had found shelter.

"That was lucky," Che said. He turned to his friends: "It was a combat helicopter, of the kind that the Americans have only used before in Vietnam. It seems they've lent a few to Tshombe's soldiers. And no doubt Tschombe's followers have also been given combat training in the United States. This business we've gotten ourselves into, it's a war by proxy between the great powers. We revolutionaries try out the latest weapon systems of the Russians, and Tschombe's guys do the same with the those of the Americans.

"Instead of focusing on liberation from all imperialists, the Africans of either side are just acting like the yard dogs of those who give them money and munitions."

After walking for some time through the dusty savanna, constantly on the watch for enemy attack, the revolutionaries were picked up by a column of trucks belonging to the Kinshasa rebels, and taken to their headquarters.

When Che was finally let in to see Colonel Sambe and presented his request for lifesaving medicines, the Colonel turned the request down flat.

"We didn't ask for you and your bunch of revolutionary Cubans. You understand nothing of our African culture, even is some of you do have a black skin, like this son of a bitch." He gestured in the direction of Che's interpreter Bramlio.

Che felt like reaching for his gun, as this insult to his loyal companion was something no Comandante of the Cuban revolution could be expected to put up with. But the barrels of half a dozen rapid fire machine guns were leveled at him, and the soldiers would have opened fire without hesitation. In the Congo at this time, a human life was worth about as much as that of a pesky mosquito. Che had no choice but to take his leave without accomplishing his errand.

For some months I had had no word of Che. This was actually nothing out of the ordinary, as the Comandante revealed his current location only rarely. Back in New York, after all, he had voiced the opinion: "Africa is one of the most important, if not *the* most important theater of conflict for the struggle against all forms of exploitation, imperialism, colonialism and neocolonialism existing in the world."

Of course he had never given up his original plan of exporting the Cuban revolution to the whole of South America. But all efforts of this kind had so far been in vain.

One of his closest confidants, Jorge Ricardo Masetti – a passionate revolutionary since the old days in Sierra Maestra – had been killed by government troops when commanding a partisan group in Argentina.

This was just one of several attempts by Che to gain a foothold in South America. So he now addressed himself to his next project – the African continent. Before this he had set up in Havana a solidarity organization of the peoples of Asia, Africa and Latin America, under the name of OSPAAAL.

In the capital of the Republic of the Congo, Brazzaville, Che believed he had found fertile soil for an African revolution. The Republic of Brazzaville had been declared – by contrast with the neighboring Democratic Republic of the Congo – a socialist state. President Alphonse Massemba-Débat saw Cuba and Communist China as his role models. Massemba-Débat lent support to a leftist rebellion which had broken out in the Republic of Kinshasa. If these rebels were successful, both Congo states could become socialist. The revolution could then spread in all directions – to Tanzania in the east, and Gabon in the west. Massemba asked Fidel Castro for support. The latter gave Che the job of planning and executing a project which was aimed at creating a new Cuba in the heart of Africa.

When an excited Che, full of revolutionary enthusiasm, had told me of his project in New York, I was again haunted by the underlying mistrust I had come to feel for politicians of every color.

Che was by this time willing to share with me all his plans for a future world of peace and justice. He was aware that I would never publish anything that could cause him any real difficulty. The fundamental philosophy of our weekly was to avoid sensationalism and all kinds of muck-raking journalism. We were a serious newspaper, and respected worldwide for our farsighted and intelligent pronouncements.

When he told me about his prospective African revolution, I asked Che whether Castro had encouraged him in this desperado undertaking, or even put pressure on him. Che declared that in the last resort he was the originator of the project. He had merely asked the Cuban government for its approval, which had not been slow in coming.

Without beating about the bush, I shared with Che my suspicion that Fidel could have seen this as an opportunity to get rid of the inconvenient popular hero of the Cuban revolution for good.

Che contradicted me energetically: "We have been training African revolutionaries as guerillas in our camps for years. All contacts having to do with trade and culture I set up myself, with major African state presidents like Ben Bella, Kwame Nkrumah und Sékou Touré. It was through my initiative that a loose alliance among the undeveloped nations of Africa came into being."

Uncle Albert entered my office in some excitement. "Monique, just switch on the television please, there's a report on the Comandante."

The screen showed a grandstand on which Fidel Castro and his brother Raúl were standing, along with some other members of the government unknown to me. On Fidel Castro's right was Che's wife wearing mourning. Castro read out Che's letter of resignation, in which he resigned all his offices as well as giving up his title of Comandante and his Cuban citizenship. It was not clear from Fidel's speech whether Che had fallen in battle, but the public reading and wording of the letter made it sound very like a last will and testament. The letter to Fidel Castro was as follows:

Havana, in the Year of Agriculture

Fidel:

At this moment I am remembering many things – for example the time when I first got to know you in the house of Maria Antonia, or when you suggested I come with you to take part in those preparatory exercises. And then all the excitement during the preparation for what we had undertaken to do, and then how one day the question was asked who should be informed in case of our death, and the way this brought home to us that this outcome was a definite possibility.

It became quite clear to us that in a revolution – if it is a genuine one – you either triumph or die. And indeed, how many of our fellow combatants failed to survive the long road to victory.

Today things seem somewhat less dramatic, as our past experiences have resulted in a process leading to maturity, but there is certainly the possibility of some situations being repeated.

I believe that I have accomplished that part of my tasks that bound me to Cuban territory and the revolution here, and so I would like to take my leave of you, my fellow combatants and your people, who are also my people.

I herewith submit a formal request to be relieved of my party leadership functions, my office as Minister, my military rank as Comandante and my Cuban citizenship. No further legalities connect me with Cuba, only ties of another sort, which can no more be sloughed off than a man can shed his own skin.

If I look back over my past life, I believe I have contributed to the victory of the revolution, and the consolidation that followed, with sufficient honesty and commitment. My only serious error, in my view, was my failure, in those early days in the Sierra Maestra, to have the necessary trust in you, and my failing to acknowledge sufficiently your qualities as a leader.

I have had wonderful times at your side, and am proud of having been part of this people in the midst of the Cuban crisis, with all the highs and lows this implied.

Rarely has a statesman been able to demonstrate his quality so outstandingly as you did in those days. I am proud to have followed you without hesitation or doubts and to have identified myself with your mindset, looking danger steadfastly in the eye and always upholding the principles in which we believed.

Now new tasks await me, somewhere on the face of this planet. I can do things that are denied to you in view of your responsibility for Cuba. And this is why it is time for us to go our separate ways.

You must know already that I feel mixed emotions on this occasion – a mixture of happiness and pain. I leave behind here my most genuine and constructive hopes, and the dearest of those whom I love. I leave behind me a people who took me in as a son, and the leave-taking pains me in the very soul. On new fields of combat I will continue to be sustained by the faith you have implanted in me, and by the revolutionary spirit of the Cuban people – as well as the conviction that I have fulfilled the holiest of my obligations, namely that of fighting the hydra of imperialism wherever it rears its ugly head. This gives me comfort and not only heals any injury, but transforms it into additional strength.

I would like to stress once more that I release Cuba from any kind of responsibility for my decisions, apart from that which results from your own example.

When my last hour strikes under foreign skies, my last thoughts will be with this people, and with you in particular. I would like to thank you for your example and your teachings, and will endeavor to remain true to my principles in all my campaigns, right down to the ultimate logical conclusion.

I have always identified myself with the foreign affairs aspect of our revolutionary politics, and that remains the case to the present day. Wherever I may happen to be, I feel that I am a Cuban revolutionary, and will continue to act as such. I leave my children and my wife nothing in material terms, which does not pain me – on the contrary, it makes me happy. I do not ask for anything for them, because I know the state will give them enough to live on and finance their education.

I could say a whole lot more to you and the Cuban people, but it is not necessary to put into words the things I would like to communicate. And I don't want to give utterance to any kind of sentimentalities. We are sure of victory. The Fatherland, or death.

With a passionate revolutionary embrace,

Yours,

Che

After this the television showed an interview with Che's father, who stated: "My son is dead. I don't know where or how he died. We have not received any word, sign of life or message, since the time of his disappearance."

Uncle Albert switched off the television and looked at me with his dark eyes, which were almost completely overshadowed by his gray eyebrows. "It seems the myth of Che has comes to an end," he said. "I am extremely sorry for you, believe me, Monique!"

"No, Uncle, the whole world is wrong about this. Che is alive – he recently sent me an emergency appeal from Kinshasa," I said, contradicting my closest relative, who shook his gray head, incredulous. "The abortive call for help emerging from the tickertape was: 'Need medicines urgently – also inhalers. Airport Kins...' – then it was broken off. On the basis of further research I was able to establish that the message should have continued as follows: 'Kinshasa and Brazzaville airports not possible to land. Closest intact airport is Pointe-Noire.' I have put together a load of medical supplies, the planes depart in two days. We will take the emergency supplies from Pointe-Noire to Madingou, as it is not far from the hospital station where Che is working as a doctor. The people there call him 'Doctor Comandante'."

"Monique, you can't be wanting to fly to Africa when the country is in the throes of a civil war! I can't allow it," said my uncle, who was so agitated that the corners of his mouth kept twitching.

To calm his nerves, I poured him a vintage genuine Napoléon brandy, which I usually kept for a small circle of special friends.

I stepped up close to him, took his hand and pressed it against my cheek. "Do you remember how you comforted me when I had torn open my knee for the second time? You went on stroking my cheek until I had calmed down."

"Well of course, you were a proper tomboy – no trees too high for you, or rivers too deep," my uncle replied. "And once you had gotten something into your head, nobody could make you change your mind. Mostly it wasn't material things that took your fancy – like expensive toys and the like – it was just your adventurous spirit demanding to get out. What worries do you think your Aunt Claudine and I had to put up with, when you and a party of school friends made that extended canoe trip on the Loire."

"But Uncle, nothing happened after all, and I'm sure it was good for my self-confidence."

"You are altogether very independent for a young woman, not in the least bit interested in the latest fashions or any of the other pleasures that Paris has to offer."

"I can only pity these silly parasitical women, who spend their inherited money or their husbands' money as if there were no tomorrow on trinkets and trivialities. I spend money too, but it makes a lot more sense to me, a thousand times more sense, to save a child in the Third World from death by starvation than to wear a sinfully costly model dress from a Christian Dior fashion house."

"Well, well, you sound just like your father – he too was just such an idealist who wanted to save the world, *ma chère Monique.* I will support your decision to take medicines to Central Africa, but only on condition that you consent to being accompanied by a former Foreign Legionary. You know Michel Sores, of course, he's a very reliable young man. His father worked here for many years, as technical director of the printing division."

I remembered this Michel very well indeed. He had been a few classes above me in grade school. When we were teenagers I had been slightly keen on him, in fact we went to the cinema together a few times, but later on we lost touch.

"I'll make a call to the American ambassador, and get

him to give you the status of a UN ambassador. The document won't protect you against violent soldiers, but the official authorities will be able to support you in case of need," my uncle decided.

"OK, Uncle, if it makes you happy, I will just have to accept a bodyguard. Though actually I can look after myself very well."

Two days later our flight left Paris for Algiers. The plane, which carried the Red Cross symbol, would go on from Algiers to Agadir and then to Dakar. In Dakar we had a twenty-four hour break scheduled, then we would go on to Abidjan, and take another break before finally reaching Pointe-Noire. Our plane was a converted military and materials transporter, which as you might expect was equipped in ancient Greek – by which I mean Spartan – style.

The six Red Cross employees, my bodyguard and myself had thus embarked on a journey where the outcome was very uncertain.

Michel Sores, whom I remembered as a carefree schoolboy, was completely changed. Not just physically but mentally as well.

Of course we were neither of us any longer teenagers, but this serious and reflective man bore no resemblance with the carefree school friend of the past. In relating to me, Michel was in no way distant or impolite, but tried to make the challenging trip as pleasant for us as possible. When he fetched me a second cup of lukewarm peppermint tea, I asked him if he had had an accident, as he dragged his left leg a little.

"Not an accident, Monique, it's a war injury I got on a mission for the Legion in Algeria."

"What was life like in the Foreign Legion? I have heard terrible stories. Are they true, or is it all greatly exaggerated?"

"The stories you hear are not at all exaggerated – government offices in France are still keeping quiet, right up to the present, about the brutality we practiced against the civil population. Whenever our group was attacked by fighters from a village, our howitzers and grenade throwers took up position in front of it and reduced the houses to rubble and ashes. Even when there was only a suspicion that National Liberation Front groups, the forces of resistance, were based in the village, we bombarded the locality with heavy weapons. This was with air support, we were backed up by combat helicopters. After I was retired from the Legion because of my wound, I went on dreaming for years about the screaming of seriously injured women and children. I had to give up my job as a garage mechanic, because I was no longer able to keep regular working hours. My orders and badges of honor – including my Badge of the Wounded, First Class, and the Legionary Cross of Honor – I handed them all back, as they would only have gone on reminding me of the murder of civilians."

"What's your life like now? Have you been able to get back anything like inner peace?"

"Oh, sure, Monique – I work in the Holy Mother Mary hospital, and live there too, in a kind of symbiosis with the Carmelite order. My work as a male nurse fulfills me completely. I've had to discover by roundabout ways that helping my neighbor has actually always been my real vocation."

It seemed like salvation when finally the word went the rounds that we would soon be landing in Pointe-Noire. As we left the aircraft in the late afternoon, the heat struck us in the face like air from a hothouse.

The entire crew were conveyed to the second best hotel on the loading area of a flatbed truck. The medicines would not be shipped until after nightfall. Early next morning, Michel and I would set off from Point-Noire in the direction of Madingou in a loaded truck. After that the Red Cross sisters were supposed to be going with us to Loubomo, so that the wounded men there could be treated. If they were capable of making the journey, they would then be carried back to Point-Noire with us.

Fortunately our accommodation offered access to a communal shower, so we were able freshen up a bit. Just seconds later we were sweating liberally again, as our hostel lacked air conditioning. The food provided was however excellent, and the service staff were exceptionally obliging.

When I told the concierge that we would be leaving at an early hour for Madingou, he looked horrified and almost begged me: "Mademoiselle, you mustn't go any further than Loubomo on any account – from there on you would be risking your lives. Marauding bands shoot at all vehicles coming that way and murder the occupants."

"But I must get to Madingou, to meet Doctor Comandante. That is where the medical supplies are urgently needed," I explained to the excited African.

When we left the next morning, the porter looked at me as if we were going to our deaths.

"Mademoiselle, take this, wear it close to your heart, it will help you." I stuffed the small scrap of cloth, which was brightly painted and set with small glass beads, into the left front pocket of my khaki shirt. Naturally I thanked all the Africans who had given us such a kind welcome.

Michel drove the truck; I sat next to him in the passenger seat, and would take over the driving to relieve him from time to time. Alongside the medical supplies, the six Red Cross sisters had created what seating they could by piling up woolen blankets and pillows, so as to get through the last phase of the journey in relative comfort.

After driving for several hours we reached Loubomo, made our way to the local infirmary station and dropped off the six sisters. There were quite a few tears shed when we made our goodbyes, as we had become good friends in the course of the journey.

We drove on for some time, along a tarmac road which gradually turned into a rutted savanna track.

I took over from Michel with the driving, so he could have a bit of a rest. The monotonous chugging of the truck's engine made me feel extremely tired, so there was a bit of a risk that I might nod off and collide with a tree. Michel gave me some lukewarm tea and a few bits of Scho-Ka-Cola.

Suddenly a few military vehicles came into sight

ahead of us. The young lads on board looked to be in poor shape. They were wearing fantastical uniforms and appeared to be rather drunk, as they kept firing off rounds in all directions with their rapid fire machine guns.

When they made signs telling us to stop, Michel yelled: "Don't stop, Monique, keep on going!" I trod so hard on the gas that the engine shrieked. The truck jerked forward and rammed the jeep that was driving ahead of us, which overturned with its occupants underneath. When the soldiers in front of us realized what had happened, they opened fire with their machine guns. Michel yelled, "Monique, keep your foot on the gas! Speed is our only hope!" At the same time he threw an old army revolver onto the dashboard, looking at me with a resolute expression which conveyed just what he meant. The last bullet left in the cylinder would have to be my salvation. He himself shot, with his machine pistol, at two jeeps which we were overtaking at headlong speed.

Michel succeeded in hitting one jeep driver and so put him out of action. But a salvo from the second jeep shredded the passenger side door of our truck, and got Michel in the chest. He dropped his machine pistol and gasped, almost inaudibly, "Don't stop, Monique, step on it!"

I floored the pedal again as far as it would go, hoping to increase the distance between us and the pursuers. Michel was by this time completely unconscious. The bloodstain on his shirt was spreading all the time. Our truck ricocheted from one side of the track to the other – so violently that I was afraid we might tip over at any moment. I reduced the speed a bit in the interest of stability. At the same time I saw that more military vehicles were coming to meet us. This threw me into panic, as I hardly thought it possible that we could escape a second time. When they came closer, I saw that the foremost vehicle had a Cuban flag on the bonnet. I called to the soldiers, "*Dónde está el comandante Che*?" – Where is Comandante Che? The soldiers saw I was driving a Red Cross vehicle, and gave me to understand that I only had a few more miles to go.

My rescuers were Cuban soldiers out on patrol, and they now proceeded to chase my pursuers. When the road widened a bit, I drove onto the right verge to see to my escort. Michel had slid down, his body lay across the passenger seat, some blood was still seeping from his wound. I fetched the first aid box, which had been stowed to one side of the passenger seat, and did what I could for Michel. His pulse was almost imperceptible.

I floored the gas pedal again, wanting to reach Che's hospital station as quickly as possible. After a few miles another track branched off. A sign with an arrow painted on it indicated that the left lane was going to Madingou. More Cuban military vehicles met me, and then escorted me back to their camp.

Arriving there, I at once tried to get medical help for Michel. A medical orderly wearing a bloody uniform and two nursing nuns helped me to lift him out of the driver's cabin. We laid him carefully on a stretcher, so he could be carried to the hospital tent.

Here the wounded were lying closely packed together on the floor. Some of them could count themselves lucky that they had a coconut mat to lie on. While he was still on the stretcher the orderly examined Michel, and the nuns took his pulse; they also held a mirror to his lips. They looked at me, shook their heads and turned away without a word.

I shouted for a doctor. I didn't want it to be true that my loyal companion had passed away.

"The Doctor Comandante is lying in his tent, he is sick himself. Have you brought the medicines he asked for?" a medical orderly asked me.

"Of course, I've brought everything. Just unload the truck, then the wounded men can be treated."

Che was lying in his tent on a coconut fiber mat, which was dyed red with his blood. His uniform was covered with bloodstains. He must have just had a severe asthma attack.

He opened his eyes, and after some reflection said: "Mademoiselle must find my appearance inappropriate. I will change for dinner. Monique, you don't need to shed any tears over me yet. As soon as I've taken my medicines, I'll be my old self again."

"On the trip here we were attacked by a trigger-happy bunch, who wounded my escort severely. He has just been pronounced dead. His courage and resolution saved my life."

"It is one of the peculiarities of this continent," Che observed, "that people who seem to be perfectly amiable get transformed overnight into ravening beasts, who stalk through the land thieving, raping and pillaging. As soon as I've recovered, I must get back to my wounded men – of course you had a chance of seeing what it's like for them.

"When we ran out of anesthetics, we gave the wounded pure alcohol before we amputated limbs. When that too ran short, we had to use any old hooch available."

"Che, I've got all the medicines you asked for. I can only hope that the exchange of fire didn't damage too much of the valuable medical supplies."

At this moment a paramedic by the name of Alassane entered the tent to give Che his medicines. "We've unloaded the truck. An initial inspection was sufficient to establish that no serious damage has occurred."

"That's one bit of good news at least. In this particular fight, success stories are a rarity," Che rumbled, trying to operate his inhaler.

"Monique, later on I'll tell you more about this disastrous military campaign in Africa."

We had to bury Michel at once, as it would have been too hazardous transporting the body back to France. Che gave a funeral address, honoring Michel as courageous Frenchman who had saved the lives of many wounded men.

Michel's grave was close to the hospital station, and was marked just by a simple wooden cross. This closed the circle, I thought, as now the former legionary would be linked to the dark continent for all time.

I spent three weeks at the Cuban base. I wrote to Uncle Albert, telling him about my new job as a nursing assistant – at the infirmary tent, every helping hand was welcome.

The two nursing sisters who had come to us from a Christian mission, with the local nursing staff to assist them, performed superhuman feats. Even more remarkable was the Doctor Comandante, who operated for hours on end. While operating he cursed the country, the people, Colonel Sambe, God and the world. He cursed and he coughed, and when he had another asthma attack, Sister Swenta rushed to Che's tent to get him his medicine.

"They must love Che a lot, although he curses all day long," I remarked to her when there was a break between operations.

"To begin with I was terrified of this guy from Cuba. Later on I realized that he is a very unusual man, with a temperament that carries him along. We all love him here at the medical station. If he didn't operate, lots of people would have died. God has given him a big heart and helping hands."

"I don't think Che has much confidence in God," I said, trying to put her right – "it's more his faith in the possibility of a socially just world."

"The people don't give a hang what motives the Comandante has for sacrificing himself here. But I am absolutely sure that even where he is concerned, God has a hand in it. When the Comandante started working here as a doctor, everyone thought he would only treat his Cubans and the Kinshasa rebels. But he helped all the wounded without exception, as well as injured civilians. When Colonel Sambe heard about it, he refused to let us have any medical supplies. Comandante Che was not deterred but just kept on working. I believe this is God's handiwork," declared little Sister Swenta bravely.

In the late evening I sat with Che at the front of his tent. In the distance we heard the cries of wild beasts, and I asked Che what he planned to do with his life now.

"This revolutionary mission in the Congo has been a complete disaster for me. Right at the start my chief of staff, Comrade Mituride, was drowned. It wasn't possible to agree on any joint military strategy with the rebel army.

"When we were engaged in combat with Belgian mercenaries and the rebels were supposed to be covering our flanks, the cowards ran away as soon as they came under fire. No Cuban revolutionary would dare to behave in such a way – with us, abandonment of your colors is subject to the death penalty. The rebel leaders sabotaged our mission right from the start. They wouldn't let me command them or give their military forces training. This Colonel Sambe is the most cowardly and the most corrupt of the whole pack of them. These shitheads won't treat enemy wounded. I insisted that at my hospital station *all* people in need of medical care would be helped – never mind what tribe they come from."

"Che, what are you going to do when you get back to Cuba?"

"I have laid down all my offices. I've never accumulated wealth. My family is provided for, I have Fidel's assurance of that. Fighting is all I can do. So I am going to get myself a well armed small unit and take the revolution from Cuba to South America. I will train the peasants to fight, and march on the capital. The country I've got my eye on is Bolivia. To begin with I am going to sound out the country and its people by entering under an assumed name. You may get the odd encrypted message from me."

"But Che, why must you always career around promoting violence? Surely your vocation is that of a doctor. You've seen how much you are needed here. In Cuba and in South America there are lots of sick people needing you to treat them. People will admire you to the limit, just as they do here in Africa."

"Monique, when I was a young man I traveled around South America with two traveling companions. Back then, we hoped for a rosy future. My comrades persuaded me one day to visit a seer. The seer was said to be descended from an Inca priest. Of course I didn't believe a word of all this hocus-pocus.

"We entered the shabby hut of this weirdo. He gave me a penetrating look, and sipped a drop of liquid from a bottle. Later I learned that this liquid is called *ayahuasca* and has hallucinogenic effects on the central nervous system.

"The seer gripped me firmly with his hand, while with the other hand he dropped coca leaves onto a plate. Meanwhile he murmured incomprehensible words continuously under his breath. After a while he looked at the plate on which the coca leaves lay, then looked at me again. Suddenly he was kneeling in front of me, and calling out over and over again, 'You are the great Son of the Sun, you are the great Son of the Sun!'

"I was taken completely by surprise, and tried to get the old man to get up, but he went on kneeling to me.

"He made me the following prophecy, in verse: 'You great Son of the Sun / liberator of all humanity / the Island of Sugar / will be your fate / no one escapes his fate / you great Son of the Sun / fight and conquer / but everywhere is treachery / even when your image / moves the whole world / you great Son of the Sun / in the old Inca kingdom / death comes to meet you / even before the dead body / missing both its hands / all your enemies shall tremble.'

"I thought at the time this was all complete garbage, the ravings of a crazed old man. But all his prophecies have come true to date. So you see, Monique, I've got to go to the old Inca kingdom."

"But Che, that would mean, surely, that you are going to meet your death. That's the very reason why you *shouldn't* go to Bolivia!"

"Monique, what does the poem say? *It will be your fate / no one escapes his fate.* Wherever I may go, my fate is fixed in advance."

"Last year we were visited by the American physicist and Nobel Prize laureate Professor John Hamilton," I said. "He gave a lecture at the Académie Française, and told us that a future technological revolution is going to change the face of the globe. He talked about 'electronic computers', so called, which will modify the traditional Hollerith punch card methods drastically. Electronic data processing will gain entry to all businesses and almost all private households. With the help of satellites stationed in the atmosphere, information will be exchanged right round the planet. Not just peaceful data, either, but including data for military purposes. Every square meter of enemy soil can be monitored. Troop movements of any kind will be exposed to early warning systems. This third technical revolution could result in a more peaceful world."

"How big is a super smart supercomputer, did the Professor say anything about that?"

"Right now he's still working with machinery that takes up about a hundred and fifty square meters. But he is firmly convinced that in a few decades there will be computers just the size of a briefcase, which will have many times the capacity of today's specimens covering a hundred and fifty square meters of ground. I just wanted to make you realize that it is something of an anachronism trying to make a revolution happen with just a few dozen armed men."

"Monique, these machines you are talking about will never completely replace the human spirit, or supersede humanity's ability to think in terms of epochs and create social justice. They will just be technical aids. No doubt a fabulous opportunity for the few manufacturers to make it big time. But I don't suppose these machines will do a thing to advance the liberation of farm laborers."

For some time we stayed drinking in the spectacle of the sunset, which every time seemed uniquely magical.

"How beautiful Africa is! And yet it's a place where

terrible crimes against humanity are being committed," I said to my beloved.

"Monique, I lean more and more to the view that these human beings, who laud themselves on their genius intellect and call themselves the crown of creation, are just one big mistake."

Chapter IX

Che sent me information on a regular basis about his revolutionary intentions. He had frequently emphasized, in talking to me, that his role as minister had never been much to his taste. He and the Castro brothers had always taken the view that the Cuban revolution should be exported to the entire South American continent. Hitherto, however, all efforts to make this a reality had failed.

In Panama, Castro's expeditionary force was taken prisoner in just a few hours. For many years Nicaragua had been ruled by the Somoza clan. Both here and in the Dominican Republic, where the wily dictator Trujillo held all the threads in his hands, the Cuban invaders experienced defeats. What looked like being the last attempt to export the revolution occurred in Haiti. The small revolutionary force was beaten again, and experienced yet another bitter defeat.

In Havana, the Castro brothers and Che Guevara remained convinced that one day their ideology would come to be adopted by other nations.

Fidel had another reason for supporting Che's activities. He had enviously looked on as the Che Guevara myth took hold of the entire planet. Che's popularity could be a threat to his own position. This darling of the people could aspire to be the Cuban number one.

Che's contacts with the People's Republic of China, and his sympathy with the teachings of the revolutionary Leon Trotsky, were a permanent irritation to Fidel.

No doubt about it, Cuba's Soviet friends looked with something less than benevolence on Che's activities, and that was putting it mildly. When Che asked for larger quantities of Chinese propaganda materials, Fidel prevented them from being imported into the Caribbean island nation.

These details I did not learn from Che of course, who still saw Fidel Castro as his friend and supreme mentor. I was told by the editor in chief of the Cuban weekly "Revolución Sí" [Revolution Yes], Marcos Sevata, who had special links with our own journal. The information was sent by a confidant of the editor in chief to our Paris post box. The journalist was one of the few Cuban representatives of the press allowed to visit both western and eastern Europe on their own initiative, for the purpose of making contact with the media there.

In this way, revolutionary Cuba hoped to make a positive impression in the eyes of the world. We for our part supplied information about the interests of our government – as well as those of friendly western nations – via a certain porter at the Hotel Ritz, who passed it on. It was always a bit of a tightrope stunt, because if we passed on anything sensational, it could be construed as an act of treason. The French government took such matters extremely seriously.

Our information was sent anonymously, and the communication was not even signed. In this way I was able to learn that Che was now in Bolivia under an assumed name. His new identity was Ramón Benitez Fernández, the fake passport giving his nationality as Uruguayan and his profession as *comerciante* or businessman.

Che had changed his appearance completely. Beardless and bald, with glasses and a belly, he looked like a well heeled bourgeois on the point of concluding an advantageous business deal. But this typical contemporary figure, with his innocuous looks, had come to Bolivia with the object of starting a guerilla war, which he hoped would not just change the face of the country but go on to engulf the entire South American continent.

With his four man strong advance guard, Che had traveled via Moscow, Prague, Frankfurt am Main and Rio de Janeiro before entering Bolivia. He trusted his faked documents and roundabout itinerary via Europe would give the immigration authorities the impression that revolutionary Cuba had nothing to do with the activities of these "businessmen". Fidel Castro had by this time made contact with the leader of Bolivia's Communists, Mario Monje. He was expected to give Che's project his fullest support.

Over the next few months, starting from November 1966, another seventeen Cuban guerilla fighters were smuggled into Bolivia. These were old comrades in arms of Che's, traveling under false passports purporting to come from Ecuador, Panama, Columbia, Uruguay, Bolivia and Peru.

One of Che's most important helpers in Bolivia was a man named Ricardo, though he had at least six aliases. With his talent for organization he had been indispensable to Che in the Congo. He now created a basis in Bolivia for the future revolutionary army.

The campaign was to be launched in Ñancahuazú, not far from Casa Calamina. The organization was strengthened with the help of an outstanding agent, to whom Che, in his coded missives, always referred as "T". From our confidential informant we learned that "T" was in fact a woman, who had been educated in Moscow, East Germany and Cuba. She was of German origin, though born in Argentina. A convinced Communist, she had studied Marxist philosophy at the Humboldt University in East Berlin, and had been Che Guevara's interpreter when he visited the city. She had worked in the past for the Ministry of State Security (the Stasi) in East Germany, as well as for the Russian secret service, the KGB. Tania was her alias, but she also appeared under a dozen other false identities. In Bolivia's capital, La Paz, she had far reaching connections, extending as far as the highest echelons of government. She had acquired Bolivian nationality by marrying a Bolivian. The marriage was short lived, however, as she wanted to be able to serve Che.

I had no difficulty imagining in what way she "served" this macho warrior, as our informant had also told me that "T" was reported to be an extremely attractive female.

Why had Che never told me about this woman? I would never have made a jealous scene about it. It had been clear to me from the start that I had no rights whatsoever where Che's private life was concerned. And besides, I hated scenes of this sort, which only resulted in mutual chagrin. Our few meetings had been such as to give us the opportunity of experiencing an episode of life, and enjoying it from the pleasant side.

But when Tania's name was mentioned, there was something quite different I could not get out of my head. Alarm bells started to ring at the idea that Che might be under surveillance by the Soviet KGB, who perhaps meant to betray or even sabotage his mission.

Chapter X

As long ago as 1959 there had been initial contacts between Bolivian sympathizers and the Cuban revolution. Castro's agents had access to the highest circles in the country.

A strike in Bolivia's tin mines was of course just what the Bolivian Communists were waiting for. They were in turn closely in touch with the Cuban guerillas.

An official protest by the Bolivian government against Cuba's interference in Bolivia's internal affairs was not slow in coming. This did not deter either Fidel or Che from continuing their underground activities against the ruling classes.

In 1964 Bolivia severed diplomatic relations with Cuba by government decree, and all Cubans were obliged to leave the country. The underground organization remained, led by a woman who later went down gloriously in the annals of revolutionary history as "Tania la Guerillera".

Che asked his contacts to find a suitable headquarters for the guerillas. This was to serve as a base camp from which to organize armed forays against the Bolivian army. Che also planned to set up a revolutionary troop which would be recruited from native farm laborers and peasants.

A suitable plot soon presented itself, located in the Santa Cruz department. The Ñancahua-zú base was situated in a gorge, masked by dense vegetation.

The Cuban agent Ricardo had acquired some three thousand acres of land for two thousand five hundred dollars. The deal was however negotiated not by him   but by a Bolivian named Coco Peredo, who pretended to be a farmer wanting to raise pigs and grow corn. The big landowner who owned most of the land in these parts was not in the least suspicious, as Coco's thorough knowledge of farming enabled him to give a convincing impression as a committed agriculturalist.

The land came with a few dilapidated buildings on it. The main building was christened by the Cubans as Casa de Calamina, meaning "house of corrugated iron". Che's group consisted of sixteen Cubans; later the team was reinforced by thirty Bolivians, three Peruvians and two Argentinians.

Just a few kilometers from the corrugated iron farm lived the former Mayor of Camiri. This inquisitive man was convinced that his new neighbors were cocaine smugglers. He demanded hush money from the supposed drug dealers, the amount of which would be based on the extent of the profits. The guerillas let their neighbor continue in his belief that they were cocaine smugglers. But as they had to anticipate unpleasant surprises at any time, caves were excavated in the mountains, in which they stored medicines, food, weapons and munitions. It turned out to be a disadvantage that the members of the group always had to march for a few hours to reach their materials. And the recruitment of new members from the poor local population proved extremely difficult. The region where the guerillas were operating was occupied by people of part *indio*, part *mestizo* origin, who had been oppressed by the rich Europeanized upper classes for centuries.

Che placed his hopes in the workers, with their trade union organization, and the cadres of the Bolivian Communist Party. But a meeting with the leader of Bolivia's Communists, Mario Monje, ended in a fiasco. Monje made demands on Che which he found it impossible to meet.

Monje was only prepared to provide guerilleros for the cause if he were to be given the military and political leadership of the movement. Che's extremely negative experience of extraneous leaders on the African mission was still vivid in his memory, so he rejected the request categorically. Basically he did not expect to find much combative spirit in the Bolivians, thinking only trained revolutionaries had any hope of success. Mario Monje left with his errand unaccomplished.

The blazing sun burned brightly in the Bolivian sky. Che had scheduled a reconnaissance march lasting several days for his group, who he feared were growing soft. Having lost their way, they had to march through impassable terrain, which made considerable inroads on their strength. At night, when they lay under the bushes, mosquitoes and ticks came to feast on the intruders. The jungle and the mountains had almost consumed the last of Che's strength. One asthma attack followed hard on the heels of the last. Eventually he sank to the ground exhausted. Only his superhuman strength of will enabled him to pull himself together and struggle onward. Their provisions were running low, so they were compelled to resort to fruits of the forest and edible roots. The poor starved packhorse, who had always loyally carried their equipment, was finally slaughtered, so that the guerilleros could have something to chew on.

After weeks of wandering aimlessly around, the shredded and tattered troop managed to get back to their corrugated iron base camp. What was worse, they had lost one of their Bolivian comrades, who had drowned in the crossing of the Rio Grande. Their headquarters was no longer secure, either, as the corrugated iron farm had been searched by the army. The wily neighbor had told the police he suspected drug activity.

Numbers at the camp had now been strengthened with the arrival of three foreigners. Tania had smuggled a Frenchman and an Argentinian into Camiri by way of La Paz. Her jeep, which she had left at headquarters, had been broken into by the police and searched. The police had found papers and photos indicating that Tania was a guerilla associate. Che had to act fast, as the Bolivian army was on their heels. In order to keep enemy patrols away from the secret depots in the caves, he laid ambushes around the main camp, which an army column walked into. The army lost seven men and fourteen prisoners. The captured men had to hand over their weapons, and then Che let them go.

The Comandante had no illusions. From now on he could not look to have a moment's peace, as the army would be on his case the whole time.

Tania, who made up the rearguard in Che's marching column, lost touch with the main group as she was suffering from flu. Her group fell into an ambush on the Rio Grande and was completely wiped out.

The thirty guerilleros were now facing two thousand heavily armed soldiers, who were thoroughly well versed in their job of combating terrorists. Moreover the army could rely on the ultra-modern combat helicopters which they had obtained from US munitions stock.

The Bolivian President had issued the order that Che was to be captured dead or alive. The blood money on his head was four thousand two hundred dollars.

The guerilleros not only suffered hunger and thirst, they also had to contend with bad weather and the jungle's thorny undergrowth.

Che's asthmatic attacks became so violent that he was now delirious, having recurrent feverish fits. His comrades laid him on a bed made up of branches and leaves. A length of tent, attached to the bushes in a provisional way, offered some shelter against the gusts of wind and the rain that pelted down on the decimated group.

Che had run out of medicine. In his delirium he was visited by the most famous revolutionaries of all time, from Símon Bolívar to Antonio Maceo. Only one failed to show up – his idol and comrade in arms, Fidel Castro.

Bolívar looked into the ravaged face of the sick revolutionary and said: "Comandante, it's a big mistake to present yourself to day laborers and peasants looking like a highway robber. Their leader needs to be a shining hero, wearing a uniform with gold braid, and he should keep a certain distance from them, because it must be clear even from a distance   who gives the orders. When you are a victorious head of state, you can play the great benefactor and spread it around. But not before, because they need to be shown unmistakably who is on top." With that the man who liberated South America from the Spaniards vanished again into the mists of history.

"My brother," called Antonio Maceo, "my heart bleeds when I look at you. South America's most important revolutionary, or the most important one in the whole world! Stand up and fight, for you are one of us. Your enemies may conquer and kill you, they may cut off your hands, but you will always be immortal!"

When Che called for his comrade Miguel, the latter heard the Comandante muttering confusedly.

"We should protect his hands," he observed to Moro.

Chapter XI

After a night of carousing, three students of the Sorbonne had broken in through the outer door of the university building and the door leading to the rectorate. In the foyer of the building they hung up a banner with writing on it and a portrait of Che Guevara. The banner bore the inscription: "The obligation of a revolutionary is to make the revolution happen!"

In the rectorate they smashed tables and a few pictures belonging to the venerable teaching institution. And the walls were defaced with Che quotations: "Let's be realistic, let's try to do the impossible!" and "Let's make two, three or many more Vietnams!"

The students Martineau Lavoine, André Richet and Jean Cluzet were quickly identified as the perpetrators, as they were boasting about their heroic exploit all over the campus at top volume.

A suit was brought against them for damage to university property, and they were expelled forthwith. Furthermore they were forbidden to set foot on university premises.

When, at our morning editorial conference, the reports of the investigating authorities were read out and the name of Che Guevara came up, it was immediately obvious that I should interview the juvenile delinquents. After considerable searching and interrogation of fellow students who were friends with the perpetrators, I found the triumvirate in a bar in the Quartier Latin. They were already in elevated mood, as they had drunk quite a few glasses of Pernod. When

I introduced myself, they became even more excited, and before anything else I had to drink two glasses of aniseed brandy with them.

"So why did you desecrate the rectorate of this prestigious university?" I asked the former students.   Jean answered immediately, without a pause for thought: "We'd been playing cards here for a few hours, and drunk a bit. Actually the whole thing was just a crazy idea."

"Not completely," André commented, "the starting point was an article in our student newspaper 'Sorbonne Today', focusing on the war in Vietnam and liberation movements worldwide."

"We were planning to organize a demonstration against the Vietnam war next week. So I had the idea that an action of this kind in the rectorate could be good publicity for us," added Martineau.

"Well, of course you succeeded in that," I put in. "But you shot yourselves in the foot, seeing that you've been expelled from the university."

"It isn't quite like that, actually – the demonstration will still be taking place, just not on university ground, and we will be there," said Martineau.

"I've studied existentialist philosophy," said André.

"Human beings are beings who are condemned to freedom, who must face up to their existence on their own responsibility. The only possibility of this lies in committing oneself totally. Jean-Paul Sartre, one of the most important luminaries of existentialism, says that we should not be trying to reach paradise in another world or in heaven, we should bring it about here and now in this society. This further implies that we must change society, and this will not always be possible without violence."

"How do you propose to bring about change, meaning revolution, here in Paris?" I objected. "The Bastille is long gone. You don't have a chance of liberating political prisoners, as happened back in 1789."

"The revolutionary handbooks of Mao Tse-tung and Che Guevara are like a leading light for us. The way Che fought fearlessly for the liberation of agricultural laborers and peasants in South America is already admirable. His conviction that America will one day be defeated is an inspiration to us. Aren't the Americans the real successors of European colonialist rule? Isn't Che right to say, 'Let's create two, three or many more Vietnams'?" demanded Martineau hotly.

"What are your concrete plans?" I asked the young revolutionaries.

"To bring about changes in this society, we still need to do a lot of work to reshape it. In Germany there are outstanding academics who lecture on this subject, as well as a progressive body of students who go out on the streets to protest against the USA's imperialist war. Their charismatic leader is a student named Rudi Dutschke. We want to sit at the feet of these progressive professors and absorb their ideas. First there is a professor in Tübingen, Ernst Bloch, who has become known for his "philosophy of hope". And then we would like to listen to the philosophers of the Frankfurt school, like Professors Max Horkheimer, Theodor W. Adorno and Herbert Marcuse," André explained.

I was actually quite impressed with what these aspiring revolutionaries had to say, and took my leave of them as soon as I could. When they wanted me to drink another glass of Pernod with them, I was able to decline on the serious grounds that I needed to get back to my editorial offices as quickly as possible, as my interview of them would be published in the next issue of Le Temps.

The taxi took me to the venerable University of the Sorbonne. Involuntarily I was reminded of my own student days. In my mind's eye I could see myself, diffident and somewhat anxious, hastening through the corridors to find the right lecture theater. When I tried to shut the heavy door of the lecture theater behind me, all my text books slid out of my hands and crashed loudly to the floor. All the students looked at me, and the professor, who was giving a lecture on the art of journalistic reporting, interrupted himself to remark, turning in my direction, that pretty students should not behave like heffalumps. Blushing scarlet, I found myself a seat, and wished the floor would open and swallow me up.

Today I was to hear world-famous Professor Olaf Carson, of the University of Uppsala, deliver a lecture on the subject, "Is there life after capitalism?" Without much in the way of preliminaries, the professor of economics tackled the question head on. His first thesis stated that in a few decades we would have a society of global citizens, and our earth would become a global village.

Conflicts in distant parts of the globe would affect us directly. The times in which it took some weeks, or even months, before you learned about wars going on at a distance were past and gone. In future any crisis in the lower zones of the global village would have immediate implications for the upper global village.

His second thesis was that under capitalism the economically strong nations have an interest in maintaining the existing system.

"In the USA it has always been taken as a given that in a situation of crisis the banks are the first thing to be saved, the people to whom the banks owe money get the short straw.

"In some states of the USA more and more people have been falling into the debt trap, being unable to pay the high mortgage rates and ending up homeless.

"In the old days you had 'debtors' towers', where poor people wasted away till they died of hunger. In England there were debtors' prisons, where so many poor people were living close packed together that they rarely survived. Rich noblemen, on the other hand, had all the privileges they could wish for to make their stay in prison a more pleasant one.

"These basic structures of financial capitalism, whereby cheated debtors are severely punished while the bank managers are rewarded, are still going strong today.

"In the USA everything possible is done to uphold the existing unjust system of capitalism. A massive bureaucratic apparatus has been set up just to forestall movements for social innovation. To maintain the capitalist system, the powers that be need the police, the news services, private security firms, prisons and soldiers. The capitalist system is based on carefully calculated pressure and clandestine surveillance. But the more this creates a climate of fear, the sooner this petrified system is going to implode. This will happen when people shrug off their fear of new ideas – the ideas which could replace capitalism.

"Only when we abandon the terrain of the markets of the past can we succeed in creating something new.

"The new markets must be demilitarized, so that a climate of trust, honor and solidarity can come into being.

"In the future global village, companies focusing on creativity and cooperation should have the upper hand. Believing Christians can call this a system of loving one's neighbor, while socialists can see the new society as an example of democratic socialism."

I found Professor Carson's lecture fascinating. The economist was firmly convinced that the capitalist system was going to be replaced, sooner or later, by a new model of society.

I would have listened to the Swedish professor for longer, but I had to get back to the office as quickly as I could, to finish my article in time for printing.

So why was Che still fighting in the Bolivian jungle against a government that was supported by American bayonets?

I could imagine what answer Che would have made. "In the future there will still be people trying to oppress and exploit their fellow human beings. If this pressure continues rising, a counterforce will develop in opposition to the despots. Our struggle here in the wilds is an example to all the peoples of this world who want to tread their own path into a liberated future.

"Every human being is a precious jewel. Every individual is in possession of a whole world of spirit, with a potential that asks to be discovered.

"One day human beings will come to realize that a new social structure can be created only when they cooperate with their fellow human beings."

Chapter XII

I was just working on an article about Che's revolutionary life to date, when my secretary placed the latest news strip from the tickertape on my desk.

"I can't making anything of these numerical combinations," she said, "but perhaps you'd like to look them over."

"It's OK, thanks, I'll see what I can do," I replied to my good-hearted Lyselle. The remark was intentionally casual. I was aware that this was a message from Che, who must be in a situation of great difficulty, as he sent this telex directly to our Paris office. Previously his personal messages had generally been conveyed by way of our secret mail box at the Hotel Ritz.

I extracted my notebook from the secret drawer to decrypt Che's column of figures. Here's the text Che had sent to me: "We are under continuous fire, Tania's group completely wiped out, we are short of medicines, weapons and munitions. Get the latest AK 30/17 defensive weapon which can bring down a helicopter. Radio contact with Cuba completely cut off. Bring materials to La Paz airport. Load onto a transport helicopter of the Bolivian army, fly it to Samaipata where we will be waiting." There followed a listing of all the medicines, weapons and munitions needed. The words "help urgently needed" recurred frequently.

At first I thought it was completely crazy, what Che wanted me to do. This rescue project struck me as totally unfeasible. Besides, the costs would be way beyond my financial means. First I got in touch with our

Cuban editor in chief, Marcos Sevata, using our secret channel. He would surely be able to advise me how this attempt to rescue Che and his comrades should be organized.

Two days later came an answer from Marcos Sevata. It contained both good and bad news. He would be able to get all the "relief supplies" needed and get them transported to the Bolivian jungle. But the costs of this "humanitarian" project would run to something like two hundred thousand new francs. Enormous bribes would have to be handed out. And it would cost a fortune to procure the anti-helicopter weapon.

A transport helicopter showing the Bolivian flag must be ready and waiting at La Paz airport, manned by two pilots. The whole risky project would be categorized as "international aid for the indigenous peoples of Bolivia".

The entire amount should be paid in dollars to a blocked account with the Bank of Bolivia in La Paz using a false name, which should sound as American as possible – something like "Rockefeller Foundation".

I did my sums and considered how I could get the money together as quickly as possible. My entire cash assets at present came to something like a hundred thousand new francs. The residual amount that was needed I would have to get from somewhere. But how? The clock was ticking.

I made an appointment with the world famous jeweler Cartier, whose business was close to the Place des Vosges. First of all I visited La Francs, our family bank, to make a few payments. I also asked to be taken to the bank's vaults, where I retrieved a small square case. I drove in my Citroën to the Place des Vosges, where I managed to find a space in the underground car park. I took the lift from here to reach the jeweler's reception area, where a lady welcomed me and showed me into Monsieur Cartier's private office.

"I'm very pleased to see you, Mademoiselle Cottillard," the proprietor of the establishment welcomed me. Monsieur Cartier was a slim middle aged man with hair graying at the temples.

Without preamble I explained to him that I needed a hundred thousand new francs at short notice, to support a humanitarian aid project in the Third World. "Mademoiselle, you uncle is very wealthy. All it takes is a word from him, and any bank in France will lend you the money," said the jeweler. "I don't want to bother my uncle with the business, as I can easily imagine what kind of negative attitude he would have to this project," I replied. "I can give you some objects as security that I am sure you will find appealing." I took from my purse the case that I had just retrieved from the bank vault, and placed it on Monsieur Cartier's desk. He opened the lid of the case, and the bright light of the desk lamp drew sparkles from the necklace, ear rings and bracelets that my mother once wore. Uncle Albert had given me the jewelry on my eighteenth birthday, saying: "You should treasure it, because not only is it extremely valuable, it is also a memento of your departed mother."

Monsieur Cartier's hands must have handled many necklaces, but when he looked at these specimens he was quite breathless. For a time he gazed almost reverentially at the content of the jewelry case, and then asked me quite shyly if he could take the articles out of the box.

"Mademoiselle Cottillard, these pieces were created by my grandfather, with his own hands. You've got flawless diamonds here, sapphires, rubies and emeralds. Today these articles are astronomically valuable. If auctioned, they might fetch a price of up to five hundred thousand new francs."

"No, Monsieur Cartier, I don't want to sell them, only to pawn them for one hundred thousand francs," I explained to the jeweler.

"I knew your brother François well. We attended the same school. Your brother was one class above me. I know the end he met, and I know what happened to your family in the war. They died for France, and no Frenchman should ever forget that.

"And for that reason, I would like to make you an alternative proposal. Take the jewelry home with you. I'll give you my check book, and you just write down whatever amount you need. You can repay me whenever you like, because my trust in any member of the Cottillard family is practically unlimited."

Taken aback, I wrote the sum of one hundred thousand francs on the check, which Monsieur Cartier had already signed. With a few words of thanks I took my leave of the kindly jeweler, and left the shop.

Chapter XIII

The small remainder of Che Guevara's group were hunkered down in the mountains of Bolivia, overgrown with impenetrable forest and undergrowth.

The Comandante, who never gave up, was now shaken by constant severe asthma attacks, so that he was no longer in control of himself and lost consciousness repeatedly.

Government helicopters flew over the mountains at all times. Moreover, Bolivian ground troops were combing the entire region around the village of Quebrada del Yuro.

The guerilleros were apathetic. They didn't even have enough cartridges left to repel the least enemy attack. All the underground fighters were in a poor state of health.

In his fever fits, Che called out to his comrades Inti and Amiceto, "We must go to Paititi, we'll be safe there!" The guerillas looked at one another; neither of them knew the place. They thought the Comandante must be having delusions. Che's fevered dreams featured an Inca priest, whose presence had a reassuring effect on him.

"You are on the way to Paititi, two more sunrises to come and then you will have reached the valley of the sun god," the priest said to him. "What is your name, wise man?" Che asked the native. "My name is Manko Ceros, and I watch over the Inca Kingdom of the Dead. You remind me of Túpac Amaru. He was a brave warrior and the last leader of the Incas, who was killed by the Spanish. By your time reckoning that was in the year 1572.

"I am come to conduct you to our Kingdom of the Dead. Do not be afraid! The native peoples await you, they will celebrate a great feast in your honor which will continue for many moons."

"Tell me something about your people," the Comandante asked the priest.

"Our people are descended from the sun god Inti. He had a son called Manco Cápas and a daughter called Mama Ocllo, who rose from the waters of Lake Titicaca. The sun god gave them the task of bringing culture and order to the scattered peoples. Manco Cápas and Mama Ocllo became a man and a woman. They wandered from Lake Titicaca to the north till they reached the valley of the Río Urubamba, where a tributary river of the Amazon has its source. When the golden rod they carried gave them a sign, they knew that was where they should settle. They were our ancestors," Manco Ceros related.

"The actual Inca kingdom was founded 1200 years after Christ. The Incas constructed gigantic terraces, slopes shaped into steps, which were irrigated by a sophisticated system of canals. They cultivated corn, potatoes, quinoa, amaranth, gourds, tomatoes, peanuts and peppers. The city of Cuzco was the political, religious and cultural center of the kingdom. This was where the rulers of the Incas resided, and it was also the place of the most important sanctuary, the Temple of the Sun. The main educational centers, the elite schools for the sons of the nobility, were likewise in Cuzco, which in 1530 counted some two hundred thousand inhabitants.

"Cuzco was overlooked by the Inca fortress Sacsayhuamán, designed to protect the holy city against enemy incursions. This fortress too, like almost all the rest, was destroyed by our Spanish conquerors. There was another fortress high up in the mountains. Its name was Machu Picchu, the mystical city. Here was the Inti Wasi, a temple of the sun, as well as the Itiwatana – a pyramid that contained a solar clock and an astronomical observatory. Then too there were the Temple of the Three Windows and the Temple of the Condor.

"The mountain fortress of Pisac was five times as big as Machu Picchu. Close to the town there was a sacred valley where only our divine kings were permitted to hunt. The town center of Pisac consisted of two parts. The one half served as living accommodation, while the other half was a sacred precinct. From the residential area a stone stairway ascended to the highest plateau. On this plateau stood our *intihuatana* or sacred stone. We had tethered the sun to this boulder, for if the heavenly body were to abandon us, the world would come to an end. The *intihuatana* was surrounded by temples, priestly palaces and mausoleums, built out of massive blocks weighing tons without the use of mortar. The entrances were designed in trapezoid form, and likewise secured with heavy stone lintels.

"But one day the Spanish aliens came, and destroyed our culture and our people. The Spanish leader Francisco Pizarro made very short work of us.

"Two hostile brothers had been waging a war of succession. As a result the Inca empire was so debilitated that we were not capable of much in the way of resistance. Hitherto unknown illnesses which the foreigners had brought with them, like smallpox and measles, sapped our will to fight still further. Moreover, the Spanish conquerors were cunning and deceitful.

"Our guileless god-king invited the Spaniards to his palace of Cajamarca, and entertained the aliens with the finest dishes and beverages. Naturally our king wanted to win the goodwill of the Spaniards for himself and his people. But Pizarro had very different ideas. He took our divine head of state captive, as well as mowing down some four thousand Inca warriors, who were unarmed as it was a time of peace.

"As a ransom, our king offered Pizarro gold and silver, as much as he wanted. We did not place such value on the precious metal as the Spaniards did. We simply saw it as a symbol representing the tears of the gods.

"So King Atahualpa ordered his subjects to procure three thousand four hundred pounds of gold and twenty-six thousand pounds of silver, hoping that then he would be set at liberty. But the conquerors had long determined that the god-king should be killed, as it would be easier to enslave the Inca people when they were leaderless.

"Atahualpa, who had first been condemned to be burned at the stake, was finally strangled on 29 August 1533. Pizarro had the cynicism to describe this impious deed as a 'mercy killing'.

"After that the bravest Inca warriors withdrew to the mountain fastness of Vilcabamba, where they organized a guerilla war against the hated Spaniards that lasted for forty years. One of the most courageous fighters was Túpac Amaru, who inflicted repeated defeats on the Spanish mounted convoys. He and his warriors seemed to have the fit of invisibility when they appeared out of nowhere and surprised the Spaniards. The stores that the conquistadors were carrying were distributed by Túpac Amaru to the people of Vilcabamba.

"But in 1572 the conquerors reached Vilcabamba and got ready to take the city. In the night before the last battle, Túpac Amaru entered the holy temple, to prepare himself for his great journey to the gods. He came to me, and together we prayed to the sun god Inti, asked him to grant Túpac Amaru peace of soul and immortality.

"The Inca warriors defended the city heroically – above all Túpac Amaru, who hurled himself at the Spaniards wielding a spear and battle axe. He killed countless Spaniards, though with their muskets and cannons they were vastly superior in fire power. Finally they made themselves masters of the last of the Inca strongholds.

"Túpac Amaru did not want to be captured alive by the Spaniards. His loyal comrades carried the severely wounded hero to the highest plateau of the city, and he threw himself from this point into the abyss.

"Che Guevara, are you ready for your soul to enter the Inca Kingdom of the Dead? Your first stop will be the Holy City of Paititi, for this was another ancient refuge of the Incas. After that your soul will be received for all eternity into the place of the gods." The wise old priest raised his hands to heaven and murmured a few words which the Comandante did not understand. "I was speaking to the sun god Inti in Quechua, the ancient language of the Incas. He is making all things ready, so that you can find peace in the Kingdom of the Dead.

"People will carry your name all over the planet, even in distant worlds your heroism will be famous – from now on you are immortal!"

Che woke up briefly and asked for water. Amiceto gave him his last sip of water, after which the Comandante went peacefully back to sleep. Now he knew the fate that was to befall him in just a few hours.

Chapter XIV

Che's guerilla group was now just seventeen men strong – though "strength" was hardly the word for it.

A guerillero who went by the name of El Chino suffered from night blindness, so that after dark they could hardly make any progress. What with hunger and thirst, the guerillas were close to desperation.

An old woman was grazing her goats in the gorge where the group were holed up, and they asked if she could tell them the whereabouts of the soldiers. But the woman either couldn't or wouldn't say. She was willing however to leave the underground fighters some food and drink. They thanked her and gave her a 50 peso bill – in the hope that she would not tell the advancing Bolivian soldiers where they were to be found.

Their hope proved treacherous, as became plain in the course of the next few hours. On the very next day, the soldiers spotted Che's small band, and hostilities commenced. They continued for some two hours. In the second skirmish Che was wounded in the leg; at the same time his gun was shot to pieces, which made him practically defenseless.

Four soldiers held their weapons trained on him, and led away the guerilla leader together with Simon Cuba Sarabia.

With his serious leg wound, Che was unable to walk. And he was again afflicted by a severe asthma attack. So the Bolivian soldiers practically had to carry their prisoners to the nearest village.

Che and two of his fellow combatants were housed

in a village school. On the following day he was inter-rogated by two Bolivian officers named Zenteno and Selich. CIA agents were also present at the hearings.

It was clear to Che from the very first moment that the interrogation would be followed by his execution.

Later he heard some shots in the adjoining room. That was where the guerillas Sarabia and Gordillo were being held. They had just been shot by the Bo-livian sergeant Mario Terán.

When Terán entered his room and reloaded his gun, Che's last words were: "Long live Cuba, long live the Revolution!"

The next sentence he spoke was cut short by a rain of bullets.

The top Bolivian politicians had never intended to give the legendary guerilla fighter a proper trial. Bolivia was a small country, and it would have been exposed to massive political pressures. These would have come not just from Cuba and its allies, but also from many western-leaning countries who might have intervened. Third World states too would have applied pressure.

So the Bolivian government kept all the journalists in the dark for weeks about what had really happened in the last hours of Che's life. Che's brother Roberto had arrived to identify the corpse. They told him that he was too late, as the military had already cremated the remains. Roberto Guevara protested in the strongest possible terms, as he and the family had wanted to say a proper goodbye to Che.

The international press likewise called for an immediate explanation of how the guerilla leader had met his death.

When the Bolivian General Ovando explained, some time later, that the body had not been cremated but had been buried in a secret location, the result was universal consternation.

A rumor got about that the Bolivian troops had cut off Che's hands, so as to make it more difficult to identify the body. The Bolivian regime wanted at all costs to avoid the Comandante's having a public funeral – whether in Argentina or in Cuba. The grave would have become a place of pilgrimage for his admirers all over the world. The Bolivians hoped that that all the excitement over the deaths of a few terrorists would die down in the foreseeable future.

The opposite turned out to be the case. When the pictures of the dead revolutionary were published worldwide, serious protest demonstrations took place in many countries.

People saw a bearded man lying half naked, with expressive dark eyes and a mouth over which an enigmatic smile seemed to play.

The dead man gave the impression of still being alive. He emanated a definite aura of immortality.

Conservative spirits like Charles de Gaulle and Bertrand Russell, church leaders like Archbishop Recife and the theologian Gonzalez Ruiz expressed their condolences to Che's brother Roberto.

Even in the United States, where the CIA was suspected of having been implicated in his death, there were expressions of sympathy for Comandante Che.

Poems were published in which Che was described as the "rebel Christ on the cross". Enthusiastic young people carried photos and posters through the streets. They gave Che the status of a newly created saint, who would be their idol from now on. European cities saw major demonstrations. Young people protested against the exploitation of the Third World, and the war being waged in Vietnam by the USA.

Among the Bolivian population, a legend acquired currency after Che's death about the revenge of the Inca priest Manco Ceros.

Almost all the officers who had been involved in Che's murder or who had given orders for it went on to die violent deaths. They were shot, or their helicopter crashed out of the skies. The peasant farmer Honorato Rojas, who had betrayed a group of Che's guerilleros to the Bolivian army, was found dead with two bullets in his head. The sergeant who had fired the shots that killed Che staggered daily through the streets of Cochabamba in a drunken stupor, before presently disappearing into a psychiatric institution.

Chapter XV

In the early hours of the morning, our passenger aircraft with propeller drive landed at La Paz airport. After passing through passport control and customs, I waited on events in the VIP lounge. As a journalist used to reporting on international conferences, I naturally had a VIP card.

Our confidant Marcos Sevata, who had been holding the whole project together from Cuba, had given me the following instructions. I should wear suitable clothes for making a half day's march, if necessary, through the Bolivian mountains. Practically no hand luggage, and a canister of water and two cans of Scho-Ka-Cola were the only supplies permitted. With three persons and all the materials we were carrying, the transport helicopter would be at the limits of its capacity.

So I changed my clothes in the ample washrooms, and let a friendly airport employee stow my two suitcases in a special luggage locker. He even asked if I wanted any breakfast. But I was so overwrought that I just asked him to bring me a big cup of café au lait. One of the pilots was supposed to pick me up and take me to the helicopter, which was waiting to leave on the airport periphery.

So I waited in the VIP lounge. From time to time I went up to the first floor, to look down through the glass at the departures and arrivals hall. Here everything was going on as usual. Travelers arrived and were welcomed by their friends and relations. Other passengers said goodbye to their relatives and hurried in the direction of the runway, where their plane presently took off and carried them out of sight. Some were still waiting in the hall for the next flight, and whiled the time away with a lemonade or ate a sandwich.

In this way two or three hours went by. I heard no word from my pilot. I couldn't ask the nice girl at the information desk what had caused the delay of my onward flight. Questions like this might have aroused suspicions and risked the failure of the entire project.

Suddenly a drone of engines was heard in the airport building. Armored vehicles drove onto the runway, and militiamen cordoned off the entire airport. Every door of the hall was occupied by heavily armed guards, who allowed no one to pass. Suddenly I heard shots, first isolated ones, then salvoes of artillery. They could be heard all the way from the end of the runway to the VIP lounge.

People panicked all over the airport. Some sought shelter under the tables, others just threw themselves down on the terrazzo floor. I hurried down to the ground floor of the VIP area, thinking I would be safer there.

I guessed that a high ranking member of the military was staging a putsch against the government, with a view to seizing power for himself. In South America, this of course would be nothing out of the ordinary.

But for my project of getting medicines and weapons to Che in response to his request, this new situation was catastrophic.

After some time a powerful explosion was heard,

and soldiers thronged into the VIP lounge. A thick-set officer with a little black moustache introduced himself as Colonel Zenteno Anaya. He asked to see my identity papers, and studied them minutely before barking at me, "Mademoiselle Cottillard, we are in the possession of multiple testimony stating that you have a connection with the terrorist leader Ernesto Guevara de la Serna. You were aiming to supply him by helicopter with weapons, munitions and medicines, so that he would be in a position to oust the Bolivian government. The Bolivian President René Barrientos Ortuño has given orders that all persons who have lent support to the guerillero Che Guevara shall be subject to the stiffest penalties. The leader of the terrorists was fatally in wounded in his last fight. Now we will proceed against those who supported him. You are a Frenchwoman. Do you know a French author named Jules Régis Debray? Have you had any contact with him in the past? Speak! If you insist on remaining silent, it could have very unpleasant consequences for you." He gave a sign, and two soldiers took up their positions to the right and left of me, with a view to putting me under arrest.

I was completely beside myself. Che was dead, my mission had failed and I myself was in a very dangerous situation.

Gradually however my head cleared. These accusations could only be a hypothesis without real proof. I could feel in my bones that treachery was at work here. I decided to go over to the attack. "Colonel, as you have seen from my documents I am a journalist with the highly regarded French weekly Le Temps, which has been carrying detailed reports about the doings of Che Guevara. The tool of my trade is the typewriter, not the machine gun.

"Our newspaper has collected funds from all over the world to help the indigenous people of Bolivia. We had purchased water purification equipment and power generators, as well as seed and medicines, meaning to transport them by helicopter into the Bolivian mountains. This mission enjoys the support of the Rockefeller Foundation and the United Nations. Let me just send a telex to our Paris office and the matter will be cleared up. Here by the way is my diplomatic card confirming that I am a special ambassador of the UNO. So you have no authority either to arrest me or to hold me against my will." The document I mentioned was genuine, as some time back Uncle Albert had obtained this diplomatic rank for me. In a dictatorship, this paper could be my salvation, he said at the time.

The Colonel was visibly surprised by my words, and replied with somewhat more restraint: "But it seems to me a little strange that these civilian articles you mentioned should have had sufficient explosive force to blow up a helicopter. When we approached the helicopter, our security forces were immediately fired on by the two pilots. We were obliged to return fire, and the whole thing went up. And once again I must ask you about your contacts with the French writer Jules Régis Debray, who is currently facing trial before a military court in La Paz for terrorist activities."

"I can only repeat that I have never had any dealings with this man," I said to the Colonel, truthfully enough.

"Mademoiselle Cottillard, I must ask you to come with me to La Paz. You will be given a suite in a hotel. We will then try to resolve this unpleasant situation as quickly as possible."

Escorted by four soldiers, I was driven to one of the best hotels in La Paz. My baggage was also restored to me, after the military had conducted a thorough inspection of the content.

"This is just for your own safety, you understand, as some enemy of the state could have concealed a bomb in your bags," the Colonel told me with a complacent smile.

Arriving at the hotel, I first took a shower, and then ordered a strong coffee from the maid. The girl, who was hardly more than a child, was insistent that I should eat something, but I resolutely declined. Freshly pressed orange juice and a bit of soda water – that was all I could handle at the moment.

They said Che was dead! I still couldn't believe it. Perhaps the military had shot the wrong man, and the Comandante was still at large in the Bolivian mountains.

It would not be the first time that a guerillero had been falsely pronounced dead. I could hear the soldiers in the corridor going back and forth in their heavy boots. Then I fell asleep. Next morning I was woken by the friendly maid, who brought me breakfast in bed on a multilayer trolley. "Mademoiselle, your really must eat something, or you could become seriously sick," the cute little girl informed me.

While I was sampling this generous repast, the telephone on my ornamental bedside table rang. Uncle Albert was on the other end of the line. "Monique, are you OK, you're not hurt?"

"My dear Uncle, I'm having a great time – I am lying here in the Hotel San Miguel and being treated like a princess."

"Thank God! Now listen, Monique: when I learned that you were being held in La Paz, I called the American ambassador. He must have contacted the American State Department. I also apprised our friend Charles de Gaulle of the situation. He called the UNO Secretary General at once. They will all be contacting the Bolivian president René Barrientos Ortuño. I am sure you will soon be able to leave La Paz. The American ambassador would like you to visit the place where the body of Che Guevara is lying in state. They would like you to identify the former Cuban Minister of Industry."

"Why should they want me, of all people?"

"You have conducted numerous interviews with him and compiled copious documentation about his career. Hardly any European journalist knew the Comandante better than you. Some of your colleagues will be present as well, but they are particularly concerned to hear what you have to say.

"After you have identified the body, you must fly to Havana, for Fidel Castro will undoubtedly be holding several days of national mourning. You might even manage to get an interview with the widow of the great revolutionary. You must warn our contact in Havana in advance, so as to avoid any holdups.   Monique, do you think you are physically and mentally capable of all this?"

"I'm doing fine, and have no doubt I can handle it," I reassured my uncle.

"My respect for you grows constantly. I look forward to being able to embrace you in Paris once more."

I thought my uncle was getting a bit sentimental in his old age.

"Uncle Albert, I love you very much. See you soon in Paris." After my uncle had given me these instructions, the call was terminated.

Reception then called immediately, asking if I could receive a visit from General Alfredo Ovando Candía.

This was quite a change of style after Colonel Zenteno Anaya. It seemed the military were now taking the trouble to be polite.

I told the head clerk at reception that I would be dressed shortly.

When there was a knock on the door I called "Come in", and several military personages entered my suite. These were just the advance guard, it seemed, an escort whose job was to hold the doors open for their superior officer. The latter turned out to be a slightly built man with light brown hair and a black moustache, wearing a more resplendent uniform than any other officer present. He introduced himself as General Alfredo Ovando Candía, Supreme Commander of the Bolivian Armed Forces.

Taking short dainty steps, he approached me and declared effusively: "Mademoiselle Cottillard, I bring you the warmest greetings from our President René Barrientos Ortuño. He asks your pardon many times for your having been placed in this embarrassing position as a result of a misunderstanding. I would also like to apologize personally for the conduct of Colonel Zenteno, whose judgment of the situation at the airport was completely misguided. He – and we – have been on constant alert for weeks, as terrorists and very dangerous enemies of state have been threatening the security of our country. As a sign of our goodwill, and by way of apology, may I present you with a bunch of orchids? It goes without saying that we will reimburse you in full for any expenses you may have incurred as a result of the sabotage at the airport.

"We will pay your hotel bill likewise. Please consider yourself as a guest of our country. I am aware that you have been asked, as the representative of your own homeland, to inspect the body of the guerilla leader Ernesto Guevara de la Serna.

"We will fly you immediately by helicopter to Bolivia's Andean jungle. A military jeep will take you on from there. After that we will fly you back to the airport in La Paz, so that you can continue your South American journey."

By this time a company of soldiers had marched up in front of the hotel, all in parade uniform. Their gold and silver medals and decorations flashed and glittered in the sun. There was a constant barking of military commands, some of them addressed to a military band. Three soldiers in full regalia held flagpoles with the French and Bolivian flags erect in their hands.

My Italian colleague Francesco Mororelli said jokingly in my ear: "Mademoiselle Monique, who's this coming on a state visit? Do you think General de Gaulle has announced himself, with a view to getting you released, or has he even threatened military retaliation?"

I wanted to answer that he was definitely exaggerating my importance, but General Ovando Candía now approached me again, offered his arm and said: "Mademoiselle Cottillard, our President René Barrientos Ortuño would be pleased if not all your memories of our country were to be negative ones. We want you to experience the friendly side of our people. It would be a great honor for us Bolivians, if you would please walk past the guard of honor that has formed up, to the strains of the Marseillaise."

I had to put a good face on it and go through this charade – otherwise my conspiratorial plan might have gone up in smoke. So while I walked past the honor guard with the general, my thoughts were with Che, whose corpse must be lying somewhere in a Bolivian mountain eyrie. If I knew Che, he would have been capable of finding amusement in this grotesque situation.

Here was his devoted assistant being forced to march arm in arm with his murderers. He would surely have been able to get something out of this situation, suggestive as it was of the exploits of Don Quixote, the knight of sorrowful countenance. The general accompanied to the door of the government limousine which was to take me to the La Paz airport.

As I drove away, the reiterated goodbyes of the murderers of Che Guevara could still be heard in the distance.

Chapter XVI

Marcos Sevata, our confidential contact in Cuba, met me at the airport in Havana with an old Chevrolet and drove me to the Hotel La Caribica.

During the drive he expressed his regrets that our joint project of providing support for Che had come to such a dismal end. I comforted him with the following words: "This was just the death that Che wanted. I think he had been waiting for it all his life, thinking that in this way he would become immortal."

Sevata had been able to make two important appointments for me – a meeting with Fidel Castro, and an interview with Che's widow, Señora Aleida March.

The following day saw a mourning ceremony on Revolution Square in Havana in honor of the fallen revolutionary leader and national hero Che Guevara. More than a hundred thousand Cubans, shattered and in tears, stood under the blazing Cuban sun to pay their last respects to their Comandante Che.

All the country's prominent politicians, from State President Osvaldo Dorticós to Fidel Castro, were present on the grandstand. Che's widow, with her children Aliusha, Camilo, Celia and Tatico, could be seen quite close to Fidel Castro. I could also make out Hilditia, Che's daughter from his first marriage. Aleida March wore a light colored monochrome dress. Her head was covered with a scarf. In the Caribbean, white is the color of mourning. Many Cuban women were wearing white as a gesture of solidarity with their dead Comandante. Through Marcos Sevata's small binoculars, I observed Che's widow, who let the whole spectacle wash over her with stony countenance.

After a few speeches by various government representatives, Fidel Castro took the stand. For him Che Guevara, he said, was the perfect expression of a revolutionary, a man with an absolutely irreproachable way of life. The Cuban head of state went on to declare: "If we are looking for a man to serve as an example, one who is not a man of our own times but a man of the future, then I can say with full conviction and with all my heart that this model is Che. If we are looking for a way of saying how we want our children to turn out, we have to say with profound conviction, We want them to be like Che!"

That was how the great revolutionary sang the praises of his soulmate. But I knew the full extent of the truth. While Che was increasingly encircled by superior enemy forces in the Bolivian mountains and fighting for survival, his boss had refused to support him. Castro should have exploited to the full all the material and propaganda resources available to him. If Che had been victorious, the Argentinian would have been hailed as one of the greatest leaders of Latin America.

Castro was aware of that. And he left his friend, who was also his competitor, to his fate.

On the following day I was due to be received by this very same head of state. Marcos Sevata had told me that the Chairman of the Revolutionary Council lived in modestly furnished premises. Only after I had been strictly vetted at the guarded entrance was I conducted, accompanied by four soldiers with the mandatory revolutionary dress, by way of a sweeping staircase to the first floor of the building.

Fidel welcomed me at the door of his office with the following words: "I am delighted, Mademoiselle Cottillard, to have the honor of welcoming you. I know your weekly Le Temps well, I read it on a regular basis, as it is one of the few western organs of the press that report almost objectively about our revolution." After a sketchy kiss of my hand, which quite took me by surprise, the Chairman of the Revolutionary Council ushered me into his office, which was furnished with a gigantic desk as well as with a large oval table surrounded by six leather upholstered chairs. He sat down on one of the leather covered chairs and asked if I would like a coffee or any other kind of drink.

I asked for a coffee, and Fidel Castro lit up one of his cigars, having asked if I didn't mind his smoking. I felt I was meeting an exceedingly polite and cultivated head of state. He didn't give the impression of being the revolutionary bruiser the western world liked to see in him.

"If you permit me, my dear Mademoiselle Cottillard, I will tell you something first of all about the present state of our island republic, and then you can ask me any questions you like."

Castro told me about the enormous difficulties the country labored under as a result of the American economic boycott.

"No North American products can be delivered to

our island. Even goods produced in other countries under US license cannot be supplied to us. Foreign ships that put in to a Cuban port are placed on a black-list by the North American port authorities, and are banned from visiting American harbors. Any American companies ignoring the blockade are subject to dra-conian penalties. All Cuba's industries are based on American technical standards. The socialist countries that support us have no spare parts for the abandoned American plant facilities. We had to switch to new units of measurement, as Cuba was used to measuring in miles and yards, but the metric system is the valid international standard. European electronic systems based on 50 Hertz won't work in Cuba, because it's always 60 Hertz here. In Europe 220 volts are stand-ard, but in Cuba it's always been 110 volts.

"The mineral oil coming from South American coun-tries has a different viscosity from the North American. Our refineries gradually broke down when we tried to process the new oil."

Fidel talked and talked. I went on taking notes. He gave me the latest production figures for tobacco and sugar. He also explained to me why he had been com-pelled to introduce food coupons for the population.

"Please write that as a result of this blockade policy by the USA, a state of war still exists in Cuba."

Fidel paused for breath, and I seized the chance to ask him a question about the death of Che Guevara. The revolutionary leader put on a statesmanlike air and told me: "We would rather have seen him as one who brings things to fulfillment, not as a combatant in the front line. But for a man with his character and temperament, I'm afraid the second path was his chosen vocation.

"We will erect a monument to Che Guevara on Revolution Square, and proclaim the day of his death a public holiday, as the Day of the Heroic Guerillero."

Now was the moment for me to address a quite particular issue in connection with Che's death. It was quite possible that if I put the question Fidel would show me the door immediately, but I risked it all the same. "In the western media, as well as in the South American press, there has been much discussion of the question whether Che's small troop actually received the support it needed from Cuba. To put it in a nutshell – did you abandon Che to his fate?"

Fidel looked at me in momentary shock, but his look was not hostile; rather his face wore an expression of astonishment.

"Mademoiselle Cottillard, I solemnly declare to you that the entire Revolutionary Council, and I too of course, had always assumed that Che would go on winning victory after victory. Here is one of his last messages, which you are very welcome to publish: 'To Comrade Fidel Castro. From the eastern part of Bolivia, where we are fighting in hope of repeating the heroic national deeds of the past, inspired by the Cuban revolution, the standard bearer of the oppressed peoples of the world, we send hearty brotherly greetings, associating ourselves thereby with the millions of people who see this date as the start of the last phase of Latin American liberation. May you, your comrades and your people receive this testimony to our unlimited devotion to the common cause, along with our best wishes!'"

Che must have sent this radio message when he was in a state of mental aberration, as it was completely out of touch with reality. My astonishment over this statement of Che's persisted a moment, so that I did not manage to ask any further pertinent questions. We just talked about a number of general problems, like standards of hotel service and the lengthy check-in procedures at Havana airport. Then I thanked him for the excellent coffee and took my leave. Fidel accompanied me to the stairs.

After this I had an appointment with Che's widow, Aleida March. The taxi, an ancient American Ford, took me to the outskirts of Havana. An unobtrusive little house was the home of the Cuban national hero. Aleida March was already waiting for me at the front door. She welcomed me with a firm handshake. Her manner was very serious. But I could see some laughter lines around the corners of her eyes, which suggested that she was also capable of being very merry. Right now, however, her beautiful eyes had dark rings around them because of the death of her beloved husband.

She invited me in and introduced me to her children. Aliusha, the eldest, was close to seven years old. Her son Camilo was five. The second daughter Celia was four years old and Tatico, the younger son, was just two. The furnishings were extremely primitive. I was of course aware that Che was averse to any kind of luxury, for himself or for his family.

After I had sat down, Aleida asked if I would like a coffee, or would I prefer lemonade? I accepted coffee, which here in Cuba was generally served black and strong, with a lot of sugar. Aleida also placed some cookies on the table. I could hear the children's voices in the next room. "Are the kids on their own?" I asked Aleida.

"No, Che's daughter from his first marriage, Hilda Beatriz, is looking after the younger children. She's a very sensible girl, eleven years old."

"Aleida – if I may call you that?" I asked her. She agreed at once. "Then please call me Monique," I said to Che's widow. "Our weekly Le Temps, let me tell you, is not the kind of gutter paper that broadcasts intimate matters to the world in garish colors. It is a serious journal which reports on global news."

"Oh yes, Che translated the odd article from your paper for me, and I was surprised at your objective reporting. You are impressively well informed about the Cuban revolution and about the role Che played in it."

At this moment it occurred to me to wonder whether Aleida could have heard anything about our liaison. She continued to chat without embarrassment, however, complaining about the western press which had always made a point of discrediting her country and its former politicians. "Monique, when Che became President of the National Bank, his enemies conducted regular campaigns against him. Not the peasants, the sugarcane workers, the poor people of the country – no, it was the landed proprietors in Cuba who slandered him and spread lies about his extraordinary achievements. The American press and the European print media snapped up these lies at once and recirculated them as gospel truths."

"Aleida, I must just come back to the time when Che was commander of the La Cabaña fortress. Were the sentences carried out by the revolutionary tribunals justified?"

"At the time I was Che's secretary, so I had a very good overview of what was going on. La Cabaña had two tribunals; one for the trial of army and police officers, the other for civilians. Che appointed the accountant Orlando Borrego as president of the court. No member of the tribunal who had suffered under the Batista regime was allowed to act as a judge. The idea was to avoid a situation where judgments would be motivated by revenge.

"Che did not take part in the trials, but handled the appeals procedure. He looked into the charge, the evidence and the verdicts. In most cases he upheld the decisions of the court.

"The death sentence was imposed on people who had tortured or murdered.

"All the statistics propagated by the US about the number of capital punishments were cooked up. In the first four months of the revolution, there were just some five hundred executions carried out in the whole of Cuba."

"Aleida, when Che was Minister of Industry, is it true that he voluntarily worked on the production line?"

"Yes, Che wanted to create the selfless citizen of the future, who would be willing to work without reservation for the good of the community. That was why he wanted to set a good example.

"Many technicians had left the island. The universities needed to train more geologists, chemists and engineers. As university studies cost nothing, being financed by the state, Che expected students to work in the vacation in factories or in farming to help out. His initiative resulted in a miraculous technological invention, a sugarcane cutting machine. Che drove the machine through the sugarcane plantations every day for a month. He had to stop frequently, as his asthma attacks were frequent and convulsive. The sugarcane workers thus saw in him a politician who was seriously committed to ensuring that conditions of work were improved. Of course they thought the world of their Minister of Industry.

"In his office, Che worked every day for sixteen hours and more. If a member of his team failed to complete his tasks in time, his salary was docked. In case of serious misdemeanors, employees would be relegated to work on the land. After a period of probation they were allowed to resume their post at the ministry.

"Che didn't want any extra remuneration as minister. He just continued to draw the salary of a Comandante. When food rationing was introduced and he found out that we were being allocated special rations, he went through the roof and insisted that we must eat just what the rationing card allowed us, like all other Cubans. Many people in Cuba admired him – he was a legend in his lifetime, and they were always wanting to do him a good turn. When we went to the cinema for instance, the girl at the desk didn't want to take money off him, but Che insisted on paying."

"Were there any serious differences between him and Fidel Castro?"

"Fidel and Che often sat up all night discussing the path Cuba should pursue on the international stage. In Che's eyes, Fidel was the boss. Within the Revolutionary Council, Fidel was always protecting Che when he wanted to go his own way or made public attacks on allied states. Without the economic help of the Comecon states, our country would have been practically finished. Fidel always reminded Che of this, when he was too inclined to glorify his revolutionary hero Mao Tse-tung."

"Aleida, I would like now to ask you a very private question, which you don't have to answer. And if you do answer, I won't publish it. The western media have carried frequent reports suggesting your husband was having affairs. How did you put up with this situation?"

"Che was a South American. It's said of them that they are rather inclined to having a bit on the side. And then the whole female world practically lay at his feet, because of his worldwide reputation. Particularly when he was away on long trips, it may well be that he didn't stick too rigidly to his marriage vows. But his family, his home – his children and myself – we were an anchor for him in the heart of a turbulent life. Monique, it was clear to me even before we got married in 1959, that I would have to share my husband with many others, because this man did so much in a relatively short time that it was as if he had lived several lives already.

I've already mentioned the fact that the western press was always trying to discredit Che. These newspaper reports were something I never really took seriously. It wasn't an issue for us either, because we were both simply happy when we were able once again to spend some time together."

Later on I took a taxi back to my hotel. I looked through the window of the car and saw people who loved life, people who bore their fate with a certain dignity even though every day was a fresh challenge for them.

EPILOG

I am sitting in my office in the Rue de Rivoli, and writing about a subject that preoccupies the whole of France like no other.

It is May 1968, and Paris is again experiencing a revolution. The Renault workers and students of the Sorbonne have joined forces and set up barricades in the Quartier Latin, a symbolic reference to the rising of the Paris communes in the year 1871. Everywhere you see pictures of Che Guevara: on the Champs-Élysées, at the Place de la Concorde and along the Boulevard Voltaire. Thousands of people are carrying Che's portrait through the streets.

On the Boulevard Saint-Michel I asked people what they thought about the young people's protest. An elderly gentleman, who gave the impression of being quite affluent, placed both his hands on my shoulders, and declared with passion: "Mademoiselle, the young people are right. Our nation is run by crazy bureaucrats who have completely lost touch with the mass of the population. These people know nothing but laws and decrees, they have no idea of the real problems suffered by the workforce. The workers must be given their due. We in France don't want to see any kind of inhuman Stalinism. But this system of capitalism, what we call the 'free world', needs to be changed. We need co-determination for the workers, and free admission of young people to the universities. Study places should not be restricted to the children of a privileged upper class. This is what you should write,

Mademoiselle!" The elderly gentleman turned on his heel and walked away.

I hadn't actually expected a reaction like that from a fellow Frenchman. I think many of the French are proud of their "Grande Nation". But on the other hand they still have something turbulent, even revolutionary in their heart of hearts.

I can well understand why they made Che into an idol.

Some days I get out the little box in which I collected Che's cigar stubs. I light a stub and play with the smoke. The Cuban cigars then give off a very special pungent scent which fills the whole room. I let myself dream, and see the Comandante standing before me, as he said with complete conviction: "Monique, one day I am going to be more famous than Jesus Christ. My appearance will be like that of Jesus Christ, and it will be so radiant that everyone else will stand in my shadow." At the time I had asked Che if he was suffering from megalomania.

Che spoke the truth. His prophecy was destined to come true. Even in the poorest hut in South America you will find a fruit crate transformed into a small altar, having its allotted place in a corner of the room. On this crate you will see the image of Mother Mary with the Child Jesus on her arm – flanked by a picture of Che Guevara. On special holy days they light a candle for the virgin Mary, asking her to protect the family and save them from suffering. And another candle will be lit for the legendary Comandante Che, who is honored as a friend, a good buddy – one who wanted to make their impoverished life better, and yet came to grief.

I have visited a number of South American countries, and have always been able to observe the ritual I have just described among poor people – and poverty in these countries is the order of the day.

No doubt Che worked successfully during his lifetime to cultivate his own myth, but at the same time there seems to be some kind of predetermination at work.

In a dark world characterized by monstrous egoism and boundless greed, the Comandante lit a light so that human beings would recognize the poverty and oppression prevailing in the Third World.

Even if our world never achieves social justice, Che will always encourage the longings, wishes and hopes of the poor and disenfranchised sectors of society.

Every hundred years a light signal is sent to us human beings from a distant planet, in hope that we will leave off our nefarious activities, as otherwise we are threatened with universal downfall. Che recognized the signs of the times, and tried to create a socially just world.

THE END

Bibliography

Ernesto "Che" Guevara
Eine Chronik [A Chronicle]
Waltraud Hagen and Peter Jacobs
Verlag Neues Leben [New Life Publishers], Berlin

Che Guevara
Mythos und Wahrheit eines Revolutionärs [Myth and Truth of a Revolutionary]
Daniel James
Wilhelm Heyne Verlag [Wilhelm Heyne Publishers], Munich

Bolivianisches Tagebuch [Bolivian Diary]
Ernesto Che Guevara
With a foreword by Fidel Castro
Munich, 1968

Worte des Che Guevara [Sayings of Che Guevara]
Edited by Alain Benoît
Frankfurt am Main, 1968

About the author

 Werner Ortmüller was born in Ebele-ben, Thuringia, in 1945. Since 1948 he has lived in Giessen, Mittelhessen. He worked as a construction engineer. For many years he was the elected workers' representative on the local Staff Council. He was involved in the setting up of various civic initiatives with the aim of promoting humane standards in municipal planning. From 1973 to 1996 he was active in local politics. A part time lyric poet, he is a member of the Karl Liebknecht Working Group, which awarded him its Peace Prize in the year 1993.

Werner Ortmüller has the following publications to his credit:

1986 *"Von Wende zu Wende" ["From Turning Point to Turning Point"]*
39 Gedichte für den Frieden [39 Poems for Peace]
Self published

1989 *Co-author of "Gegen den Strom" ["Against the Current"]*
Poems
Publisher: Peter Bernhardi

1992 *Co-author of "Religiöse Judenfeindschaft" ["Religious Anti-Semitism"]*
Documentary
Publisher: Peter Bernhardi

1997 *"Leben wird Sarajewo"* *["Life Becomes Sarajevo"]*
Poems
Publisher: Frieling-Verlag

2002 *"Friedenstaube sterbenskrank"* *["Dove of Peace Sick to Death"]*
Poems
Publisher: R. G. Fischer Verlag

2003 *"Flammenzeit"* *["Flame Time"]*
Poems
Publisher: Verlag Ehgart & Albohn GmbH

2005 *"Marsschatten"* *["Shadow of Mars"]*
Poems
Publisher: Books on Demand GmbH

2005 *"Sabi. Das Elfenmädchen"* *["Sabi, the Elf Maiden"]*
A children's book
Publisher: Verlag Ehgart & Albohn GmbH

2007 *"Hindukuschtod"* *["Death in the Hindu Kush"]*
Poems
Publisher: Herbert Utz Verlag, Munich

2011 *"Er nannte mich Ami-Boy"* *["He Called me a Yankee Boy"]*
Novel
Publisher: Deutsche Literaturgesellschaft, Berlin